A. M. NEILLY AND
M. R. NEILLY

WOLF ISLAND MYSTERIES II

Wolf Island Mysteries II
Copyright © 2023 by A. M. Neilly | M. R. Neilly

All rights reserved. No part of this publication may be reproduced, distributed, or transmitted in any form or by any means, including photocopying, recording, or other electronic or mechanical methods, without the prior written permission of the author, except in the case of brief quotations embodied in critical reviews and certain other non-commercial uses permitted by copyright law.

Tellwell Talent
www.tellwell.ca

ISBN
978-0-2288-9043-0 (Hardcover)
978-0-2288-9042-3 (Paperback)
978-0-2288-9044-7 (eBook)

Thanks to you, the reader.

CONTENTS

Chapter 1 1

Chapter 2 3

Chapter 3 5

Chapter 4 9

Chapter 5 17

Chapter 6 19

Chapter 7 22

Chapter 8 29

Chapter 9 32

Chapter 10 36

Chapter 11... 38

Chapter 12 44

Chapter 13 48

Chapter 14... 51

Chapter 15 54

Chapter 16 56

Chapter 17... 57

Chapter 18	59
Chapter 19	61
Chapter 20	69
Chapter 21	73
Chapter 22	78
Chapter 23	84
Chapter 24	87
Chapter 25	91
Chapter 26	99
Chapter 27	102
Chapter 28	107
Chapter 29	111
Chapter 30	114
Chapter 31	122
Chapter 32	124
Chapter 33	126
Chapter 34	129
Chapter 35	133
Chapter 36	138
Chapter 37	144
Chapter 38	146
Chapter 39	150
Chapter 40	154
Chapter 41	158

Chapter 42	161
Chapter 43	164
Chapter 44	167
Chapter 45	172
Chapter 46	174
Chapter 47	176
Chapter 48	179
Chapter 49	181
Chapter 50	183
Chapter 51	189
Chapter 52	197
Chapter 53	199
Chapter 54	202
Chapter 55	205
Chapter 56	208
Chapter 57	211
Chapter 58	213
Chapter 59	216
Chapter 60	219
Chapter 61	221
Chapter 62	228
Chapter 63	230
Chapter 64	235
Chapter 65	237

Chapter 66	242
Chapter 67	245
Chapter 68	246
Chapter 69	247
About the Authors	249

CHAPTER 1

A BLEAK, ORANGE SLIT OF light on the horizon heralded a new day, but just barely. The grass was still wet under foot and cloaked in impenetrable black shadows. A new moon meant that it was almost impossible to see.

On a hill above the town of Milford, three dark shadows stood very still, as if frozen. They appeared out of nowhere, in the middle of the road. No one was around, no one to witness a cruel mission on this lonely country road.

There were about a dozen cows in a nearby field, and they were turning their backs and starting to saunter away from a large pond.

The figures stole over the fence and began to assess the large animals, their size and weight. The dosage depended on it. This finished, they huddled together, communicating without uttering a sound.

The cows became nervous and began to low. They kept moving. Instinct was telling them to put some distance between themselves and the intruders. In a few minutes, lights appeared in the distant farmhouse. Already a dog could be heard, barking. It seemed to be heading their way.

One of the figures broke away from the others and approached the pond. He withdrew a small vial from his pocket and emptied the contents into the water, returning to the others just as the dog came upon them.

The old dog bared his teeth. He barked and snarled. His job was to protect the herd. Hackles raised, the brave animal stood its ground in front of the intruders— he was determined to drive them off.

The strangers circled around, then moved slowly forward, backing the dog against the fence.

Shouts echoed across the field. Lights played along the ground. Someone was coming.

The farmer and his two sons looked everywhere for the dog. They called and called, but it had vanished.

CHAPTER 2

THERE WEREN'T MANY SATURDAY MORNINGS when you were lucky enough, or early enough, to score a booth at the popular *Porthole* snack bar. Rebuilt, modernized, slick black and grey walls, barn board here and there—the cheesy nautical theme was gone at last. People rallied around the owner and patronized the Porthole every chance they could. After the fire last year, Rod, the owner, joked wryly that the place had been built on an aboriginal burial ground and that the place was cursed. Judging by the crowds though, it wasn't much of a curse. Usually, the place was so crowded that Darcy and his friends would take their orders to-go and sit on one of the picnic tables out front or park themselves at the end of the pier.

The coolness of a late summer's morning would soon give way to a swelling yellow sun. Darcy glanced at his watch. It was an old Seiko, an analog diver's watch with luminous numbers and hands, passed down from grandfather to father to son. It didn't display a heart rate or GPS co-ordinates. It wasn't paired to a cell phone. No Bluetooth. Old school, people would say when they saw it: it just told the time. It was his first watch, signifying a coming of age, of responsibility.

Luckily, Darcy managed to be one of the first through the door. He grabbed a booth and was now sprawled out, back against the wall and legs stretched along the bench seat. He watched Rod move quickly about the kitchen. It almost looked like he was breakdancing: two hops to the right: the grill; one to the left: the toaster and bread; up for the plates; down for the eggs and milk.

While Darcy kept an eye on the goings on behind the counter, off in the corner at a small table, a man in dark glasses was studying Darcy. Nobody had taken any notice of his erect posture, his hands concealed beneath the table.

Darcy glanced down at his order number again, eleven. He had ordered the Porthole breakfast, his favourite, with of course, "Don't tell me," Rod said, with a look of disapproval, "chocolate milkshake, right?"

"Eleven and twelve!" Rod called out, before turning back to the grill.

The man in the corner moved quickly, arriving at the counter just ahead of Darcy. As he reached over Darcy's tray for his own, he inverted a tiny vial over the milkshake. A single drop fell.

Back at his table, the man sat down, just long enough to see Darcy take a gulp of his drink. Then, without even pretending to touch his food, he got up and left.

Later, one of Rod's servers checked around the room for the customer who had departed without eating a single bite of his meal. She shook her head in dismay. *What a waste*, she thought to herself as she took the tray away.

CHAPTER 3

DUSK. THE SUN WAS SETTING now, and he had idled around the entire island. Was it unfinished business that had brought Darcy back? Even in the encroaching darkness, he could see the yellow and black signs warning people off the island. He recognized the symbols for toxic chemicals, the skull and crossbones. He smiled to himself. The government didn't miss a trick. They didn't want visitors. It seemed like overkill for keeping people away from a wrecked power plant. Still, he had seen the drums full of chemical waste for himself. Whatever the story, he had to admit that the signs worked. A shiver ran down his spine.

Darcy had completed the trip around the island. He had advanced the throttle of his wooden, 1960s hydroplane, leaning forward to compensate for the upward pitching motion of the bow, when he caught sight of three bright lights hovering over the island. Without thinking, he throttled off too abruptly, and, too late, water flooded over the back of the boat, threatening to sink it.

His father's voice rang in his ears. *That motor is too big for this tiny boat, too heavy. You'll see.* And he was right. He was going down if he didn't do something. The boat was sluggish, and water sloshed around him. He mashed the throttle to the firewall and accelerated hard, heading for the moonlit shoreline, and beached his craft.

Darcy climbed out of the waterlogged cockpit and immediately began to shiver. He scanned the skies above the island. The strange lights were gone. The air smelled as it did after a thunderstorm, fresh and clean.

Standing there, hands on hips, he took stock of his position. He recognized the beach. He recalled their escape from the old power plant, down a dark tunnel, with the alien sphere lighting the way. That was almost a year ago.

* * *

He snapped out of his odd reverie and glanced at his watch. Ten o'clock. How was this possible? He had lost time, at least an hour or more. Try as he might, he couldn't recall.

In the soft, blue light of the moon, Darcy seized a flashlight from the cockpit and strode up the beach and into the woods. He knew where he was going. It seemed like only yesterday that the teens had emerged from there, through a steel hatch in the middle of nowhere.

In seconds, he was down the ladder and standing in the tunnel. He had a vague recollection that the army had welded the hatch shut, but this thought floated briefly across his mind and disappeared.

Moonlight shone down from the open hatch and this made it just possible to see where he was. Darcy switched on the flashlight and paused. Cobwebs. *There hasn't been another person down here in months.*

Off to the left was the corridor that led to the old power plant, or what was left of it after its demolition. To the right, there was an eerie feeling of something trying to pull him forward. He stood there for a full two minutes, his hand frozen to the ladder. It was warm in the tunnel, yet goose bumps had formed on his arms, and a cold chill ran up his back. He could stay where he was forever, nervous and afraid, but no, that wasn't who he was. He let go of the ladder and forced one foot in front of the other, his flashlight illuminating the way ahead, until he reached what appeared to be the end of the tunnel. From there he could see five dark shafts radiating in various directions.

What now? Darcy asked himself.

He stepped back quickly, realizing that his imagination was running amok. "Okay, get real," he said aloud. "There's nothing here."

With his arm outstretched, he aimed his flashlight into the first tunnel, straight into darkness. It was the same for the next three. The fifth was odd. He stepped forward just a few feet when the hair on his arms stood straight up. Static electricity, he assumed.

A thought sprang into Darcy's head, or was that a whisper? *You should keep going. What would it hurt to go a little farther, maybe ten more steps?* It wasn't logical. Logic would have told him that ten more steps would have returned nothing of any value. Logic would have said that disembodied voices counselling him weren't possible when you are all alone in a tunnel. Now he couldn't stop himself. His hand tightened on the flashlight: if need be, it would make a good weapon.

His footsteps resonated down the shaft. He had a bad feeling that he might be followed, and in a moment of panic, he spun around. Nothing but dust particles suspended in the waning gleam of his flashlight.

The main tunnel was well out of sight now, but something was still pushing, or pulling, him forward. He wasn't thinking straight. *One more minute,* Darcy thought, *and no matter what, that's it.* The walls of the shaft were hewn out of solid rock. *Smooth to the touch.* As he went along, he wondered where he was relative to the lake. Was he directly under the lake now or maybe under the island?

Another question arose: why was this part of the system unfinished, with no lights, no ventilation? The sound of his footsteps, which at first echoed forever through the empty expanse, seemed to tighten up.

Suddenly there it was, something dark and menacing, huge. It came up from the floor and loomed over him. It was grinning at him, and for the first time in his life, Darcy was utterly terrified.

CHAPTER 4

DARCY AWOKE WITH A START, disoriented. Light was streaming in through a window. He squinted his eyes, which finally focussed on the glowing numbers of a digital clock. 11:48 am. *Huh?*

It was hard to think. His t-shirt was damp with cold sweat, and he was freezing. He raised his head a little and looked around. He was at home all right, and this was his room and his bed. It had only been a dream, but a very real, disturbing one. *Wasn't I just at the Porthole this morning? Why am I in bed during the day?*

Now something more urgent was happening. A loud gurgling sound and severe cramps made him clutch his stomach. *Gulp!* He rolled out of bed and ran for the bathroom, where he dropped to his knees and grabbed the sides of the toilet bowl. His stomach heaved as he vomited, so hard that it splashed back up into his face. He threw up repeatedly, with strong stomach cramps alerting him each time.

Afterwards, weak and exhausted, he collapsed onto the cold bathroom tiles. It felt like his throat was burning, and the taste in his mouth was disgusting. Worse still, he was too afraid to move, even to rinse out his mouth or to wash his face. His body ached all over, and the cold bathroom floor wasn't helping. One minute hot, the next, feeling like he was freezing, he dragged a towel from the rack and pulled it over himself. He could see his warm bed beckoning to him, just a short distance away.

Darcy remained where he was until he could stand it no longer. He got to his knees, but a wave of nausea hit him and kept him down. It would be another hour before he tried again. Eventually, he crawled to the side of his bed, pulled the heavy quilt off and wrapped it around himself. Had he ever felt this cold before? And that dream, it certainly hadn't helped. It felt so real that he wondered if this wasn't just another part of it.

Returning to the bathroom on all fours, he curled up on the bathmat in front of the tub and covered himself with the quilt. He tried to sleep, but the rumble in his stomach and a number of nightmarish images persisted. This flu, or whatever it was, was giving him vivid hallucinations. Was he still in the dream? Was it a warning?

Hours later, the queasiness subsided a little. Deciding to take a chance, Darcy pushed the quilt aside and slowly sat up. *So far so good*, he thought as he crawled back to his bed and warily climbed in. More than anything, he wanted sleep, but it eluded him. Frustrated, he stared up at the ceiling. Perhaps being sick made him hallucinate, or maybe it was because he hadn't been able to stop thinking about last year and the bizarre events that took place on Wolf Island. Maybe this is where the dream came from. He wondered if Logan and Ben had had any dreams, surely Logan must have. Not that he would tell anyone. Most guys wouldn't. And certainly not him, he'd never admit it unless one of them admitted it first.

Darcy usually tried very hard not to let his thoughts wander to John McCarthy and Ed Harris. *Where in the universe they could possibly be?* This was a question that he couldn't answer and one that made his imagination reel. Still, he needed to keep his mind off the nausea that lurked in the background. He forced his mind back to that time, when Logan's grandfather and Mr. Harris were abducted…by what looked like an alien tractor beam. The media had reported that the men were dead, but that was what the army wanted everybody to think. He could not shake the image of the two men being drawn into a giant wormhole of some kind, lifted right off the ground and pulled by a peculiar gravitational force, and in an instant, gone.

Where were they? Where had the aliens taken them? What did they want with them? Was it all about the sphere and its unlimited power? Grisly thoughts from his imagination had been tormenting him every week since it happened. Experiments, torture—were they being dissected? The mind can be a terrible thing, manufacturing outcomes far worse than reality.

At last, a wave of exhaustion overcame him and he slid into a deep sleep.

Hours later, he again awoke with a start. Now it was night. *How long was I out?* he wondered. He glanced at his watch.

The avalanche of thoughts resumed. If it hadn't been for Gerard Bloch, the lunatic CEO from Globicon, none of this would have happened. All of it was the fault of that man, he just had to have what the sphere possessed, unlimited power, and he was ready to do anything to get it. Even more troubling, what were the aliens doing with it, the ones who had taken John and Ed?

No, stop, Darcy chided himself. He didn't want to think about this anymore. What he needed was some fresh air.

Raising himself to a sitting position, he swung his legs over the side of the bed. *So far so good*. He took a chance and leaned over to grab his running shoes. *Whoa, okay, not a good idea*. A bitter, burning taste surged into his mouth. *Okay, no bending over*, he told himself as he rolled back down. If he stayed here, he could probably lift his legs up one at a time to put his shoes on. That worked, he was *half way there*. Darcy rolled his head to the side, spotted his jacket and dragged it toward him. It was time to try sitting up again. Raising himself as little as possible, he struggled into his jacket and wrapped the blanket around his shoulders.

"Okay, here goes," he whispered as he struggled to his feet. Standing, he felt weak and wobbly. Good thing his desk was beside his bed, he made a grab for it to steady himself. Closing his eyes didn't help. He'd need to wait a few minutes until things settled down.

After a while, he was able to step up onto the chair, turn and sit on his desk. The lightheaded feeling subsided, and he swivelled around to face the window. It made barely a squeak as he pushed it up all the way. He made sure to keep his head up and this stopped the room from spinning. He crawled out the window onto the roof over the garage, dragging the blanket behind him. The roof was almost flat here. He could stretch out his legs and lean back against the wall of the house.

The cool, evening air felt good and in no time, it started to clear his head. For some reason, Darcy always felt better out here. He could feel himself relaxing. After a few minutes, he reached back through the window and grabbed his phone from the desk.

There was only one person he could talk to.

"R U awake?" the text read.

Almost immediately came the response, "Yeah, give me a call."

Darcy paused for a moment and smiled. His phone rang.

"What's happening?" a familiar voice asked.

"Not much, Logan," Darcy lied. There was no way that he was going to whine about being sick. "I'm on the roof. I was just thinking, wouldn't it be great if I could just stay up here, maybe even sleep out here?" He was tempted to tell Logan about his dream, but changed his mind.

"Yeah, there's a great idea," Logan laughed, "as long as you don't roll over in your sleep. It's a long way down."

"Nah, the worst that could happen is I might get a bush in the face." Darcy laughed.

"Or," Logan pointed out, "you could get hit by lightning."

"That'll never happen."

"Famous last words."

"Isn't that what your grandfather used to say all the time?" Darcy said.

"Yeah, he did, every time we thought we had a great idea."

Darcy regretted bringing up John McCarthy and changed the subject. "Hey, do you know what I love about being out here? It's the way I can see for miles and miles in every direction. Tonight, it's really clear. I can even see all the way over to… Hey, wait a minute! There are some lights over there!"

"Over where?" Logan was curious.

"Over on Wolf Island," Darcy's voice dropped to a whisper. "I wonder what's going on."

"Probably a bonfire. Maybe somebody's having a bush party?" Logan suggested.

"No, can't be," replied Darcy curtly. "Nobody goes over there anymore, and anyway the lights aren't on the ground, they're in the air, just above the trees. They seem to be circling the island." He recalled the dream. Was he back in the dream?

"Oh, probably a small plane or a helicopter," Logan answered as he tried to stifle a yawn. "Maybe the military is keeping an eye on the place. It wouldn't surprise me."

"Hmm…maybe, but they're kind of zigzagging around, that's… Wait! They're moving up now, really fast," Darcy whispered.

Logan could hear a shuffling noise over the phone as Darcy scrambled to his feet.

"Wow! They just zipped up and now they've stopped dead. There are three of them! They're hovering there! This is… okay… Wait, they've started to move again. They're heading east…WHOA! What the …? They're gone! Disappeared! Honest, in like a split second! Nothing can move that fast."

"Right," Logan grunted, "you're putting me on. Nice try, buddy!"

"No!" Darcy asserted in a loud whisper. "I'm not kidding. Honest, you should have seen it."

"Okay, well, I guess this proves the military is still hanging around. They probably have some helicopters over there," Logan decided.

"Helicopters can't move that fast," Darcy insisted. "I'm telling you, one second, they were there, and then *BAM* they were gone. I've never seen a helicopter move that fast, have you? And it couldn't have been a plane because planes don't hover."

"Yeah, some can. I've seen them on television," Logan lowered his voice. He could hear his parents coming up the stairs.

"Yeah, I know about them, but you don't actually think they'd have any of those things hovering over Wolf Island, do you? I think I'm going to tell Ben about this," said Darcy, a trace of irritation edging his voice.

"Listen okay, I believe you," Logan reassured him and paused. "Not everyone would, but I do. Crap, I have to go. I have a feeling my mom will be checking to see if I'm asleep. Funny, I've been looking after myself for three weeks while they were in Africa. Now they're back and checking on me."

He paused. His tone changed. "Could you tell Ben that I have something I want to remind you guys about? There's something that we forgot."

"What'd we forget?" asked Darcy, his interest piqued.

"I'll see you tomorrow. I'll show you."

"Okay, sure. Call me," Darcy said, ending the call.

He sat down again, back against the wall and pulled the blanket up to his chin. That dream was so real, and there was no doubt about the tunnel being real. He was the last one to climb out last year and he was sure that something wanted to lure him in. It gave him the chills just thinking about it.

He wanted the nightmare to end. Had it really ended though?

Not far away, on the other side of Milford, someone else was watching the skies. They too had seen the lights.

CHAPTER 5

THE GLINT OF HIS BINOCULARS was still visible despite the new moon. Corporal Stanley was camped on the mainland, east of Wolf Island. His orders were to monitor the island for strange activities or visitors. It was boring as hell, but it took him off the base and certainly away from the city. The air smelled clean, sweet even, redolent with poplar and cedar. Since he had arrived a year ago, he'd grown accustomed to fishing off the pier, but not in uniform. This was a covert operation.

He knew he wasn't fooling anybody though. Even with his hair a little longer, and the civilian clothes, his perfect posture and referring to everyone as, sir, or m'am, pointed to military. Still, folks never bothered him and he'd even struck up a friendship with a few of the locals. "Yoga instructor?" they'd ask with a wink. "Right!"

"Okay, you got me, I'm a spy!" This was closer to the truth, but it brought even more laughter.

After two tours in Afghanistan, he was anxious to adjust to civilian life. Once an army sharpshooter, he was used to observing for long periods of time without moving a muscle. Sitting on a deck chair and sipping on an iced tea was a sweet assignment. And if this job meant blending in and reading mystery or spy novels on the beach under a blue, summer sky, well, it was okay with him. His superiors were aware that he needed some quiet time and a good rest. He'd earned it.

In his favourite position, with a perfect view of the island and its surroundings, the corporal drew a deep breath. It was dusk now and there was a velvety, tropical quality to the air, infused by fresh water, lake water. He knew its dewy sweetness. The island had settled into a black shadow on the lake.

Something caught his eye. He sat up, more alert. He held his breath. Of course, he'd heard the stories about Wolf Island. Part native legend, part modern myth blended with alien technology and corporate greed. It was no surprise that the army was watching. For the most part, the threatening signs posted on the beach did their job and people stayed away. His shift was almost over and he would continue surveillance from the comfort of his rented cottage by the shore, using night vision cameras. Now something stirred.

Three lights, an intense whitish-blue, rose up into the sky and shot directly overhead to the east. He'd been around aircraft all his life, but he'd never seen anything like this. For a time, he couldn't move.

CHAPTER 6

IT WAS STILL EARLY MORNING. Logan was straddling his bike, standing in front of his grandfather's old farmhouse, frowning as he stared up at the place. The windows were dark with no curtains. The birdbath was gone, and the flowerbeds were overgrown with weeds. It looked like nobody had been there for a very long time.

Logan shook his head. He felt guilty that even he had only been back a few times, and only to help his dad tidy up and sort through the things that weren't broken. Over the past few weeks, while his parents were in Africa, he had come to cut the grass but hadn't gone inside.

Barn swallows twittered in the distance. The damp of morning still clung to the surrounding fields of corn and hay. It was a wonderful view. So easy to understand why his grandfather had loved the place.

Logan turned away, lowered his bike to the ground and pulled out his phone. Holding it tightly against his ear, he stared intently at the lilac bushes across the road. Hidden right there, on the other side of those bushes, was the reason he'd come.

Four rings and his phone call went to voice mail. "Listen, Darcy," he almost whispered, "can you meet me at the farm house? I thought maybe we could retrieve a few things." Ever since last summer he wondered if someone might be listening in on his conversations. *As if whispering to his friend would make it harder for them*, he thought, laughing at himself. "Oh, by the way, can you bring your fishing rod case? I need to borrow it."

He left a message for Ben as well and climbed the old, cracked cement steps to the porch. The two matching chairs were still there and between them stood a small, white, wrought iron table. He stared at the scene for a moment before lowering himself onto the top step: this had been his spot when the two old men entertained him with stories about their travels.

Logan suddenly became very anxious to have another look at those plans, the ones that Grampa had made and hidden one year ago. He thought that they must be for something very important, which made it weird that he and his friends could have forgotten about them! In the chaos of last summer and the many interrogations by the army, a strange fog had settled in his mind. He couldn't explain it.

Now the fog had lifted. For a reason he couldn't fathom, an urgency to find out what happened to his grandfather consumed him. He knew how desperate that idea sounded, but he didn't care. Even if recovering the container was risky, he had to do it. He had a feeling that this was what his grandfather was referring to in that last phone call, a call that should have been impossible: *There's something you need to know!*

Logan was just sorry that he'd wasted so much time. Now he had to think carefully. What would be the best way, the safest way to retrieve it? He considered for a moment. Why would they care about him and his friends now?

Still, he refused to be reckless, to just march over there and dig it up. He needed a plan. He had learned the hard way that some things concerning his grandfather could be downright dangerous.

He shook his head. *Come on, I'm being stupid. There can't be anything to worry about now, not after all this time.* He narrowed his eyes and scanned the surrounding area. Nothing stirred. Everything looked normal and ordinary. *There!* He reassured himself, *I'm all alone, absolutely nobody around, and the only sounds are the birds.* Still, a nagging thought persisted: *Isn't that what they'd want me to think?*

CHAPTER 7

IT WAS ALMOST FORTY MINUTES later when Ben cycled into the driveway, followed a few minutes later by Darcy, who seemed uncharacteristically out of breath, but had remembered the fishing rod case. The chill in the air was giving way to a fuzzy warmth. Logan peeled his jacket off and tied it around his waist.

"What's up?" asked Ben. "Why were you whispering on the phone? Did something happen?"

"Yeah, I remembered something," Logan spoke quietly to his friends, who were huddled close together on the driveway. "First, did Darcy tell you? He saw lights on Wolf Island last night."

"No! A*bove* Wolf Island," Darcy corrected. He gave the black fishing rod case to Logan.

"Great, thanks, this is just what I need," Logan casually slung it onto his shoulder. "I don't know about those lights though," he shrugged, "I'm still not really sure it wasn't the military. I mean it could have …"

"Oh, come on! No way that was the army," Darcy interrupted, sounding frustrated. He turned to Ben, gesturing with his hands, "Listen, these lights were darting around, really fast, like they were looking for something, then they slowed way down and formed a triangle, just above the trees. Next thing I know, they shot way up and stopped dead. And just like that… poof," he snapped his fingers, "they disappeared. Do you know of anything that can do that?"

"I don't know, maybe a new kind of helicopter?" Ben shrugged.

Darcy scowled. *Where had he heard this before?*

Ben continued, "On the other hand, now that we actually know that aliens exist, maybe they're back on the island."

"That's right!" Darcy pointed a finger at Ben in a triumphant gesture. "Think about it. Maybe they've come to get *us* this time. After all, we know about the sphere, too. Logan actually held it in his hands. Maybe they need you, or all of us, to get your grandfather to do something for them. I'll bet you anything that those lights were *them*."

"Okay, okay, anything's possible," Logan conceded, "although I don't know why they'd wait a year. Anyway, I vote we go over there this week and investigate. We can take my grandfather's boat. Maybe we can find the place where you saw the lights, but right now, there's something we have to do, something important." Logan winked at the two of them and gestured for them to follow. "Come on."

"What for?" Darcy asked, as he fell in behind Logan. "Where are we going?"

Logan didn't answer. Ben shrugged.

Coming to a halt at the edge of the road, Logan tilted his head toward the far side, indicating a spot.

"Ben, have you forgotten what's buried there?" he asked, as he watched Ben's face.

Immediately Ben's eyes lit up. "For real?" He was now wide-eyed and grinning. "I thought about that stuff a while ago, but I figured you'd probably already dug it all up, that is, if the army didn't get them."

"Geez," Darcy looked around sharply, "have you checked already? Do you know for sure if it's there? I could have sworn the army found them. You know, after your grandfather and Mr. Harris disappeared, when that army general came back here to search the property again. Those soldiers had shovels. They were digging everywhere around the place."

"Yeah, they were looking for diagrams or notes or anything about the sphere, but I'm pretty sure they didn't find the plans. How could they when they weren't even on the property?"

The boys were standing in a circle, still at the edge of the road. Logan now looked worried. "At least I don't think so. Why would they look over there? I didn't see them do that. Did either of you?"

Darcy spun around and began to march over toward the bushes, "Come on," he called over his shoulder. "Why are we still talking? Let's check it out!"

"No!" Logan grabbed Darcy by the arm, jerking him around. "We can't go over there, not without a plan. No kidding, I wouldn't put it past the government to keep on eye on us."

"That's right!" Ben was rolling his eyes skyward as he confronted Darcy, "For all we know, there could be a drone up there right now, watching every move we make."

The others glanced up nervously.

"Anyway, it's not up to you and me," Ben continued, "Logan will have to figure out what to do with them. They belonged to his grandfather."

"I already know what to do. I've been thinking about it," Logan informed them. "We have to find out what those plans are for, and since none of us will ever have a clue, we need to give them to..."

"Hey," Ben raised an eyebrow and scowled as he interrupted Logan, "we can't do that!"

With his hands on his hips, Logan stared at his friends for a moment before continuing. "Don't you guys remember how complicated the plans looked? I only know one person who could probably figure them out. Besides, they're not even mine, my grandfather left them for my dad, remember?"

Darcy didn't seem to hear. He was shifting back and forth, hands in his jacket pockets. His thoughts were far away.

"You can't tell your father," Ben said in a nervous voice.

"Yes, I can, I have to tell him. Who else is there? Remember, you said it was up to me. This stuff belonged to my grandfather, and now they belong to my dad. He was supposed to find them, not us."

"I know, but how can you do that? What are you going to say? You know the whole thing will come out. Oh, by the way, Dad, Grampa left these plans for you, he hid them from the army and that crazy dude from

Globicon. Oh, and by the way, did I mention that we've been lying to you because we were threatened by some scary guys? Guys who don't want anyone to know that Grampa is still alive, just taken away by some aliens. Yeah, that's right, he's on another planet somewhere, but he wanted you to have these. Can you figure out what they're for, please? We'd really love to know!"

"Yup, that's right, only we don't even know if they're still there. Let's check it out first." Darcy nudged Logan's arm. "Is that old football still in your grandfather's garage?"

"What's that got to do with anything?" Ben asked, with some sarcasm. "Great time for a game of catch, right!"

Logan shook his head. He didn't like the part of referee and chose to ignore the remark. "I don't know. It might be. Why, what are you thinking?"

"We just need it for a few minutes. Let's find it." Darcy grabbed Logan by the arm and began to pull him up the driveway.

The old garage had two wooden doors. As Logan yanked one open, it screeched in loud protest. Ben squeezed his eyes shut at the sound, "Oh good, I bet they could hear that all the way to the lake."

"Don't be so paranoid," Darcy grumbled.

The garage had been tidied up since the last time the boys were there. Although Logan's father had thrown a lot of things away, it was still half-full of cardboard boxes that were now neatly organized against the back wall.

To Darcy's relief, the football was sitting atop the nearest box. He snatched the ball and spun around quickly. "Think fast!" he yelled as he threw the ball toward Logan.

Logan ran out onto the driveway and caught it after the first bounce. "I hope you know what you're doing because I don't have time for this," he said in a loud whisper. He lobbed the ball back.

"Uh-huh, I know. Now, I want you to go for a *long* one," Darcy gave Logan an intense look. "A *really* long one," he pointed toward the road, "*if you know what I mean.*" His eyes kept darting toward the bushes across the road. "And if you don't catch it, you'll have to find it." There was almost a singsong quality to his voice.

"Yes!" Logan yelled, beginning to laugh as he headed toward the road, the fishing rod case still slung over his shoulder.

He paused as an old, red pickup truck passed by, giving him a wide berth. Logan waved at the driver. Red tail lights well in the distance, Logan ran to the far side of the road with his arms out, waiting for the pass. The ball spiralled high over Logan's head and landed on the other side of the road behind the bushes. Logan jumped the ditch and plunged head long into the bushes.

"Oh, right!" yelled Ben as he smiled back at Darcy, "Wait up Logan, I'm coming to help!" Ben had finally caught on to Darcy's plan. He jumped the ditch and scrambled over some old farm fencing, hot on Logan's trail.

The pair disappeared into a thicket of lilac bushes and began to search around for any bare spots. If they thought this was going to be easy, they were mistaken: any trace of their digging last year was covered in dead leaves and weeds.

"Do you see it?" yelled Darcy from the driveway.

"Not yet!" Logan called out from the bushes.

Darcy began to pace. A few minutes passed. *Maybe the army had found the cooler and its contents after all.* Darcy rubbed his eyes before squeezing them shut—they had started to water and sting. He dug his fingers into his shoulder, massaging a sudden, sharp pain. For some reason throwing the ball had made his shoulder hurt. *Crazy.* A shiver ran up his back. He was having a flashback to the nightmare, that weird feeling down in the tunnel, something wanting to pull him into the darkness. What he needed was to get home.

"That's long enough," he muttered. "I'm coming to help!"

CHAPTER 8

A FOOTBALL SHOT OUT FROM the bushes, high over Darcy's head, and bounced on the lawn behind him.

Covered with dirt, but looking very pleased with themselves, Ben and Logan leaped the ditch and jogged across the road, coming to a stop a few feet from Darcy.

"So did you find it?" Darcy asked. "Is it still over there?"

"Yup, we've got it!" beamed Logan, as he patted the fishing case slung over his shoulder.

"So, that's why you wanted the case," Darcy grinned. "Good one!"

"I thought so. I thought of it on the way up here," Logan said. "People are always fishing around here, so I doubt anyone will even notice."

"And that was a pretty smart idea with the football," Ben conceded. "But if nobody minds, now that we have *you-know-what*, I'd like to get out of here. Remember, eyes in the sky." He glanced skyward to emphasize the point.

There were nods all around.

"I need to get home," Darcy agreed. He was still feeling lousy.

"By the way," Ben continued, "I know it's not that important, but the skull is still there. I saw the plastic container."

The *skull*, it was the skull of a sabre-tooth cat, no less. Logan winced. The skull was what had led them to the videotape and finally to the sphere. He remembered when he'd first sought the help of Professor Prentiss, a man he thought he could trust. The memory still haunted him. The professor had revealed the secret of the sphere to the CEO of Globicon, hoping for recognition and funding, but instead put his own daughter in mortal danger.

Logan shook his head unconsciously. "Leave it there. It's too big and I'm not sure what to do with it yet."

"So what are we going to do now?" Darcy asked. Despite his warm jacket, he was shivering. "Um, are you really going to give the plans to your father? Don't you think that could get a little tricky?"

"I guess, but he's the only one who might be able to figure them out." Logan shrugged, "I'll just have to say we found them."

Ben shook his head. "I still think this is a really bad idea. How is he going to believe that we found them in a place that was searched, how many times, by the army?" Ben held up his hands. "Oh, wait a second, I just had an idea. Why don't we tell him that we found them at the bottom of the lake? At least that would be the truth. We could say that we were just minding our own business, fishing, and what do you know, we pulled up a trunk that just happened to belong to your grandfather! Wow, talk about a weird coincidence!"

Logan patted Ben on the head. "Very funny buddy, but how stupid do I look? I'm going to tell my dad that Darth dug them up." Logan was referring to Grampa's dog. "He knows Darth loves digging stuff up. My dad will believe that."

"Sounds good to me." Darcy had wrapped his arms around himself. His teeth were chattering.

"Yeah, every time he comes back here, he tries to bring something home with him." Logan laughed. "Last time it was a tree branch. You should have seen him. He dragged it all the way back to my place. He even growled at me when I tried to take it away from him!"

"I guess Darth still misses your grandfather," Ben added, before turning to Darcy. "Hey, how come you keep shaking? It's not cold."

"Maybe not for you," answered Darcy. He was shuffling from one foot to the other; his eyes were red and glassy. "I think I might have caught the flu. Or maybe it's food poisoning."

CHAPTER 9

As they raced down the hill toward town, two cars sped by, going the opposite way.

The drivers glanced in their direction, but didn't seem interested. Remembering the events of last year, Ben returned their gaze.

The driver of the blue car kept his eyes on them in his rear-view mirror. *Huh, clever kid*, he thought. *He's suspicious. We'll have to be careful.*

"No, nothing," he reported to the person on the other end of the call. "They were just horsing around. They didn't even go into the house"

The boys were four blocks from Logan's house, when they left the road and headed into the park. It was a short cut that they always took: it would bring them out at the end of Logan's street.

"Hey," Ben shouted, "I guess your parents are home now?"

"Yeah, got back last night," Logan answered. "I only saw them for a couple of minutes. I'll bet they're still jet lagged."

Darcy was breathing hard, struggling to keep up.

"Where did they go this time?" Ben asked.

"Africa," Logan said. "They went to see a cave that was supposed to have alien bones inside."

"No kidding? That would be really something. I hope they got there before some government guys found the cave and grabbed the bones." Ben was smirking now. "Anyway, I guess it wouldn't matter, would it? The government would have taken the bones from your parents and told everyone that they belonged to some animal."

"You're right. The bones went missing. The man who guided them to the cave said he saw the bones himself."

"He was probably…ah… telling the truth," Darcy was breathing heavily. The rotten feeling in his stomach was back and getting worse by the second.

"Yeah, well, I'm surprised your parents went away at all after what happened last year!" Ben said as they turned onto Logan's street. "They weren't even on the plane before your grandfather was kidnapped."

"Yeah, and that's why this time they asked Mrs. Sandluck to check up on me every morning," he explained.

"Geez, I'd hate that," Ben said. "It's like having a babysitter."

"Nah, it's okay. Mrs. Sandluck is pretty cool. She brought me hot cinnamon buns every morning. The part I didn't like was that my dad asked Chief Bailey to look in on me. He stopped off every day on his way home from work. He kept trying to get me to go to his house for dinner. I started to wonder if the Einhorns were making up weird stories about me again. I swear I live next door to a pair of psycho stalkers."

"Yup, they're weirdoes. But maybe, if you stopped robbing banks and breaking into houses," Ben joked, "they might leave you alone."

"Yeah," Logan laughed, "I'll think about that, if it isn't too late. You know, by now the whole neighbourhood probably thinks I'm a criminal, because of the police car in my driveway every day."

"Hey… guys?" Darcy's voice was weak and sounded strained. He had slowed down, unable to keep up. "I don't think I'm…"

Logan and Ben had just turned into Logan's driveway. They looked back just in time to see Darcy veer off the road and collapse onto the neighbour's front lawn.

By the time they reached him, Darcy was curled up and holding onto his stomach. His face was twisted in pain. He groaned and rolled from side to side.

Logan and Ben crouched beside him.

Darcy's eyes rolled up into his head. His face turned beet red, his jaw was locked.

"What the hell is this? What's going on here?" Logan's neighbour, Mr. Einhorn, yelled as he marched toward them, waving them away. "I want you kids off my lawn!"

"Can't you see he's sick?" Ben shot back.

"Right, probably drunk," jeered the neighbour. "You kids! Get him off my lawn before I call the police."

"No!" shouted Logan. "He's sick! Call 9-1-1!"

Einhorn paused and stared at them with scorn. He wasn't going to have any kid telling him what to do.

Ben had been staring down at Darcy. He could see the pain on his friend's face. Anger and shock had momentarily paralyzed him. Still, he rummaged through his pockets in search of his phone. Logan glanced up when he heard Ben ask for an ambulance.

Darcy shook violently, there was foam oozing from his mouth.

Einhorn jumped back a few feet, "He's having a fit," he said in a shaky voice. "I'll bet he's on drugs. You kids are always taking drugs!"

Logan ripped off his jacket and wrapped it around Darcy to keep him warm. *This can't be happening*, he thought. *Why did Darcy look like he was going to die?*

CHAPTER 10

"One minute Darcy was riding along, the next he was on the ground, shaking," Logan explained, his voice cracking with emotion. Darcy's mother was crying softly while his father tried to comfort her. They were crowded into one of the hospital waiting rooms. Logan and Ben had called their own parents, who came right away.

"Darcy just said he was cold. I remember his teeth were chattering. He thought he was catching the flu or something," Ben said quietly.

The worried questions kept coming until a doctor appeared in the doorway. Dr. Wendall was tall and athletic looking. Her blonde hair was pulled tightly back, giving her a somewhat severe but professional appearance. Her hands were in fists, pushed deeply into the pockets of her blue scrubs.

Everybody jumped up. "Mr. and Mrs. Ryder?" she asked.

Darcy's parents took a step forward but not too close, respecting social distancing measures, a decent six feet.

"I'm his mom. Please tell me he's going to be okay." Mrs. Ryder's hands were trembling. As she spoke, she dabbed at her wet cheeks with a tissue, her eyes were red.

"I don't understand any of this. He was fine this morning. What could have happened?"

Mr. Ryder was studying the floor as he rubbed his forehead. His impatience had morphed slowly into anger at the lengthy wait for news; and though he wouldn't say it aloud, he wondered if his son's condition was the result of drugs. For a few years now, he'd been hearing some stories from a few of the parents he worked with.

"Yes, well, these things can hit you pretty quickly," the doctor said. "We're still running tests, but presently we believe it's more than likely a virus or it may even be food poisoning. We've stabilized him. You can go in and see him in a few minutes."

She paused and glanced at Mr. Ryder, "The good news is that the toxicology screen came back negative. Whatever your son has, it wasn't a result of drug use." Another pause. "The nurse will come and get you in a few minutes," the doctor smiled and left.

A nurse with a clipboard entered the room. A man in dark clothing and sunglasses brushed against her as he left. The nurse gave him a strange look as he left. *Really dark glasses*, she thought to herself, *that's odd*. The thought briefly flickered in her mind and was gone. She walked a few more feet before stopping to look around. "Could I please see the parents of Darcy Ryder?"

After a brief introduction, she said in a hushed voice, "Before you see your son, could you answer a few questions? It's important that we know where Darcy has been and what he's had to eat or drink in the last twelve hours."

CHAPTER 11

IT WAS EVENING. THE DAY was beginning to cool, the sun well past its peak. Logan and his father were sitting at the kitchen table. A shaft of soft light shone through the drapes and lit the dust swirling in the air. His mother was making tea.

"Do you think Darcy's going to be okay?" Logan asked.

"Oh yes, I'm sure he'll be fine," answered his father.

"Of course, he will," his mother said. "He's young and strong," she continued, her voice a bit too loud.

"Tell me where you were today," his father asked as he eyed his son. There was tension in his voice. "You're not feeling sick or anything yourself, are you?"

"No, I'm good," Logan gave his best convincing smile. "We were just at Grampa's house, and we never ate anything. The only food I had was this morning before I left."

"What were you doing at your grandfather's place?"

"We were just checking the place out, that's all," Logan replied, "And by the way, we found something up there, something Darth must have dug up. It's a steel tube. It looks like there might be plans inside."

"Plans... you mean like blueprints?" At once, Logan's father seemed interested. "Where are they? They have to be Dad's. Did you bring them home? Let's have a look," he said.

Before Logan knew it, the plans were spread across the table. Coffee mugs, salt and pepper shakers held down the curled corners.

"This might be interesting," she said as she raised her eyebrows. Her husband and son were already completely absorbed. She smiled to herself and took a seat on one of the bar stools to watch.

"Again, where did you say you found these?" Scott had begun counting the number of pages.

"Darth dug it up. It was buried at the side of the barn." Logan watched his father's face change.

"Did you say buried?" Now Scott was staring at his son.

"Yeah," Logan nodded, "weird, huh?"

Logan was studying his father's expression. How much easier would it be if he could just tell his parents the truth? The real story of how he'd gotten the tube, how his grandfather had put it in an old army trunk and dumped it into the lake. He'd have to be careful, one thing could lead to another, and before he knew it, the whole story could come out. How would his father feel about Grampa being alive but not on this world?

He wondered who his father would believe if he blurted out the truth. There was his word, but the army had produced a body, and there were doctors and a few experts who had all testified that Grampa had been crushed when the roof of the old power plant collapsed.

"So, um, why do you think he buried the plans?" Logan asked his father.

Scott was leaning over the table when he looked up. "You must remember what he was like, what a secretive person he could be. I know he was brilliant, but certainly some of the things he did could be called, well, eccentric to say the least." Scott stared down at the plans again, "Even so, this does seem a little extreme, even for him."

Cathy was getting a kick out of watching her husband and son, how intrigued they were with John McCarthy's plans. She loved a mystery. She was dying to participate. *No, she thought, this will be good for them, a chance to do something together. Maybe Logan will finally talk to his father about whatever was bothering him.* His grandfather's death was bad enough, but she was sure that there was something else. Something he was hiding.

For the rest of the evening, Logan watched his father carefully go over the plans. He became excited as he ran his finger across one sheet and onto the next. Sometimes he would look surprised and he would mutter under his breath. At other times, he scratched his head looking confused.

It was after 11 o'clock when Scott finally collapsed into a chair. He slumped forward with his elbows on his knees and rested his chin in his hands.

"What is it, Dad?" Logan asked. "Can you tell what it is?"

His father looked tired, still suffering from jetlag as he leaned back in his chair, "Parts of it I understand, but as to its function, I haven't got a clue. And then there's the power source."

"What about the power source?" Logan had been standing this whole time; now he slid into the seat across from his dad.

"It doesn't seem to have one," his father shrugged. "And I can tell that whatever this thing is, it's going to need a big one. There must be more plans somewhere. We need something to explain how your grandfather intended to power this thing. And above all, we need to know what he had in mind when he designed it."

Logan shrugged without looking up. He was a terrible liar, but at least he wouldn't be lying about this part. "Honestly, Dad," he began shaking his head, "that's all that was in the tube. Did Grampa have any secret hiding places?" prompted Logan. "Do you remember anything like that?

Scott shook his head. "Not that I can remember."

"Well, what about Globicon?" Logan's mother was watching her husband from the doorway. "Didn't that psychopath, the one from Globicon, didn't he take all of your grandfather's files and journals? Do you think that when the company was forced to return your father's belongings, they decided to keep something?"

"Oh, I think it's a safe bet they did," answered Scott, "but if my father was smart enough to hide these drawings, you can bet that its purpose and power source are hidden as well."

"You don't have any idea where he might have put them?" asked Cathy.

"No, no I don't," Scott yawned, "and right now I'm too tired to think. Sorry." He patted Logan on the shoulder. "What do you say we pack all of this up and go to bed? Maybe I'll be able to think better in the morning." He got up from the table and leaned against it for a moment, staring down at the plans.

"Don't worry about the plans, I'll put them away," Logan volunteered. His father smiled and mussed up his son's hair, as if in thanks, and ambled over to the stairs.

Logan carefully stacked the sheets in order. He rolled them up tight, tied them with the string his grandfather had used and slid them into their plastic sleeve, returning them to the metal tube.

"I'm putting this back in the fishing rod case," he called after his parents, who were at the top of the stairs.

"Good idea," his father called back. "And will you do me a favour, Logan? Take Darth out for a walk."

Logan stashed the fishing rod case in the top of the hall closet before whistling for Darth. He pulled his phone from his pocket. As he led the dog out the front door, he checked his messages. There were two, one from Ben: *Can't believe what happened. Hope Darcy is okay. He never gets sick. What's happening with the plans? Did you show your father?!!!* The second from Katy: *Just got back. I'd really like to see you. My Dad is working on his new boat tomorrow. I'm helping. Do you want to meet me at the marina?*

He texted Ben first: *My parents think Darcy will be fine. He's a pretty strong guy. Yes, Dad looked at the plans, but he can't figure out what Grampa wanted to build.*

It was all he could do not to respond to Katy right away. He was relieved that she didn't know about him riding by her house every day; it meant that he could pretend to be surprised by her return. He wondered what he would say when he saw her.

As Logan stepped out onto the porch, he noticed the coolness of the night air and decided to duck back inside for a jacket. When he returned, he realized that he'd lost sight of Darth. Being a black Labrador retriever meant that Darth was almost impossible to see in the dark. Logan hustled down the brick path to the sidewalk, where he stopped to look around. Finally, Logan spied Darth in the neighbour's yard, nose to the ground, following a scent.

"Hey, buddy!" Logan yelled. "What are you doing over there?"

At that moment, a man on the opposite side of the street stepped out of the darkness and started to run. He had been out of sight until now, standing under a tree. At the corner, the stranger paused and glanced over his shoulder.

Logan noticed something very odd about the man: even though it was very dark, he was wearing sunglasses. He watched the man enter the park under the streetlight and disappear along the path. It suddenly seemed very quiet. The only sound was Darth's heavy panting.

CHAPTER 12

THE FOLLOWING DAY WAS WARM with a slight breeze, a perfect day for cleaning a boat. The marina parking lot was almost full. Katy Prentiss was leaning against her father's car. She was waiting for the boys. Her father had arrived a half hour earlier.

That morning, Logan had been lying in bed staring up at the ceiling. While he loved the idea of spending the day with Katy, he was torn. With Darcy in the hospital, he felt guilty about doing anything enjoyable. It was difficult to get the images of what his friend looked like, lying on the grass, sick and in pain. In the end, his mother had reassured him that Darcy was probably fine, undergoing tests and not receiving visitors until later in the day. With a clear conscience, Logan texted Katy that he was on his way.

"Actually," his father had caught him at the door, "if you're going to the marina, can you check on your grandfather's boat?"

This made Logan feel better about going, there was a reason to go now. He wheeled his bike from the garage, and minutes later he was at the marina. Ben arrived a few seconds later.

"Darcy's still sick," Ben called out as he pulled into the parking lot and jumped off his bike.

"What did you hear?" asked Logan.

"My mom has a friend at the hospital. She said they're still checking him out," Ben answered. "His parents are there right now, but she said it would probably be okay if we go over after dinner."

"Great," said Logan. "Do you want to meet me there?"

"What's wrong with Darcy?" Katy had come up beside Logan and hugged him affectionately from the side.

"They think he might have a virus, or it could be food poisoning. He's in the hospital—he passed out on my neighbour's lawn." Logan explained as he pushed his bike into the bicycle rack.

"Yeah, and old Mr. Einhorn thought he was on drugs," Ben said with some disgust. "You should have seen the dirty looks he gave us. He wouldn't even call for an ambulance. I had to."

"The doctors pumped his stomach," Logan added making a face. "They put a tube down his throat. But I'm sure he'll be better soon."

"Wow, I'm surprised. I didn't think Darcy ever got sick," said Katy. "I hope he's okay. Can I go with you tonight?"

"Sure," nodded Ben, "do you want to meet us at the hospital?"

"Hey, what's the hold up? Come on you guys, I could use a little help!" The professor was waving at them from the catwalk.

"Okay, but wait a minute, I want to get a drink. I'll be right there." Katy started to search for change in her backpack when Logan handed her some coins.

"You should get yours first," he said as he leaned against the side of the machine. Katy stepped in front of him bringing a whiff of lavender to Logan's nostrils. The smell instantly brought back last summer and the beginnings of his deeper feelings for her. He took a small step closer and let the fragrance drift toward him. *Nice*, he thought as he smiled to himself, feeling himself sink into that moment.

The hiss of a soda can being opened startled Logan, who was searching for change as Katy turned toward him. "Um, I think I'm going to get a root beer," he said turning to the machine. "So, do you want me to text you before I leave for the hospital?"

"That would be great, thanks." She smiled at him and that made him blush.

Katy bowed her head and pretended not to notice. She liked him and she didn't want him to be embarrassed.

At the boat, the professor had propped open the engine hatch. Katy and the boys dropped their backpacks and placed their drinks on a picnic table nearby.

"I told my dad that I would help clean the boat. I thought maybe you guys wouldn't mind helping. Dad says he'll buy us hotdogs at the *Porthole*."

"That sounds good to me," Ben replied, relishing the thought.

"Yeah," Logan agreed. "Anything involving food sounds good to you."

Katy unlocked her father's locker to retrieve the cleaning supplies. Ben and Logan were a step away against a wall. They were trying to stay out of the way as people streamed past them.

Ben flinched—his head was giving off a warning signal— the buzzing that he hadn't felt in almost a year was back.

CHAPTER 13

Ben looked around, but there were just too many people. Everyone with a boat was at the marina that day, so it was hardly surprising when no one took any notice of a man strolling by in dark sunglasses.

The man paused at the end of the picnic table, propped a foot on the seat, seemingly to tie an errant shoelace. Hidden in the palm of his hand was a tiny vial of dark liquid. With his back to the boys, he shook a few drops into one of the drinks. A moment later, he stood up and adjusted his glasses. Without a look back, the man proceeded along the catwalk to the end, where he blended deep into the shadows.

"It looks pretty good, don't you think?" said the professor, stepping back with some admiration in his voice. "You guys did a nice job cleaning it up."

"Guys, Dad?" said Katy. "Really?"

"It does. It's a really nice boat," Logan agreed. He cast an envious glance in its direction.

Sleek, modern and fast, neighbours who knew the professor would later say that his boat was a "mid-life crisis" purchase, an attempt to recapture his lost youth. *Undignified*, another would say. Black from bow to stern, with white leather bucket seats trimmed in red pin striping and a fully digital, black light illuminated instrument panel, the boat seemed totally out of character for a man of the professor's age and profession.

"He bought it last year," Katy added. "Just after…"

"Hey, Katy, I really think you should be out of the sun, you've already had too much today. All of you really," the professor called out.

Katy's father was a cautious man. He wore a wide-brimmed hat, sunglasses, sunscreen daubed on like war paint, long pants and a long-sleeved shirt. He could have gone all day without the hint of a tan.

The professor thanked the teens for their help and gave some money to Katy.

Logan decided it was time to do what his father had asked, to check on his grandfather's boat.

The *Disco Volante* was just a little further along the catwalk. With its tarpaulin on, it looked almost lonely sitting there. There were long cobwebs from the dock to the boat, and a fine layer of dust everywhere. Logan's father had been too busy for fishing this summer, or maybe he just didn't feel like it anymore after Grampa was reported dead. Whatever it was, the boat had sat mostly unused over the summer.

When it came to this particular boat, Logan couldn't help himself. He pulled back the tarp and climbed into the driver's seat. The boat was rocking gently and Logan had his hand draped over the wheel. Ben and Katy climbed aboard.

"It must be so hard not to tell your dad that his father is still alive, somewhere," said Ben.

"But you can't tell him!" Katy said urgently, as she moved forward and climbed into the passenger seat. "And it's not like anyone will ever see him again, right? I mean, who knows where he is?" Katy was waving her hands about as she talked. "And anyway," she finished, "would your dad even believe you?"

"Yeah, I know," agreed Logan. "I won't say anything. It's just that I'm tired of lying."

"What do you think those army people would do if they found out that we told somebody?" Ben whispered as he leaned forward. "I'll bet you anything they could make us all disappear. Isn't that what they did with Bloch? I doubt if anyone will ever see that guy again, right?"

It was hard to forget that image, the Chief Executive Officer of Globicon, Gerard Bloch, gone stark raving mad and taken into custody by the army that summer night, amidst the flames, the military and … the sphere.

"Okay, that's it!" Katy had covered her ears. "That's enough, I'm leaving now," she said. She jumped up and stepped out of the boat.

Standing above them on the catwalk, she crossed her arms and began to tap her foot impatiently. "Food, you guys. Remember? No more scary talk, okay? Let's just go and get something to eat."

"You're right," Ben conceded. "Sorry!"

Logan had one foot on the catwalk, just as his phone rang. When he glanced down, something made him lose his footing.

CHAPTER 14

Ben grabbed him by the arm to stop him from falling.

"Look, look at this, it's the same as before!" Logan was wide-eyed as he regained his footing and held his phone in front of Katy's face and next in front of Ben's. "See, remember? These are the same symbols we saw when my grandfather tried to call me after he was taken!"

"So answer it!" Ben pushed the phone back toward Logan. "See who it is!"

"Hello?" Logan said cautiously. "Who is this?"

The sound was garbled. "Pa…poor…reception… ground," said the voice, "come…me…at Wolf…land," and then nothing.

Katy had put her head as close to Logan's as possible. "I heard that. You don't think that was your grandfather, do you?"

"I'm not sure. It could have been. It sounded like him," Logan looked confused.

"I thought I heard 'Wolf Island'. Whoever it is wants you to go there, right?" asked Katy.

"You can't go, it wasn't him. How could it be?" asked Ben, who had taken a step back. He was shaking his head. "Somebody just wants to get you alone over there, probably that general and those army dudes."

"This doesn't make sense, okay, it's creepy," Katy was glaring at the phone. "Your grandfather is out there, someplace." She jabbed her finger toward the sky, "Why would he tell you to go to Wolf Island?"

"I don't know, but I really think it could have been him. I need to know." Logan put the phone away and strode toward the parking lot.

"Where are you going?" Katy called. She and Ben grabbed their backpacks and followed behind.

"Don't you see?" Logan swung around to face them at the edge of the parking lot. He held his phone up. "I want to know where those symbols came from. Who could do that? Who could make them the same as when my grandfather tried to call me? Nobody knew about that call last year, except us."

"Yeah, but maybe the army has a way, and they're...," Ben started to say, before a loud car horn drowned him out.

"I said move! Are you deaf, or what?" shouted an irate driver. He'd been blocked in. He couldn't back up and he couldn't go forward. A girl on a bicycle was sitting in front of his car. It was odd the way the rider was just looking around, oblivious to the noise and the angry driver, who was now waving his arm out the window. Finally, the car door swung open and the driver jumped out. Logan rushed forward to grab the handlebars; he pulled the bike and its rider far enough forward to allow the car to leave.

"Stupid!" the driver yelled as he jumped back into his car.

"Why didn't you get out of the way?" Logan asked. "That guy was really ticked."

The girl said nothing. She just stared past Logan to Ben.

Katy hadn't moved. She was watching the girl's strange behaviour. Not as tall as Katy herself, the girl was dressed very oddly. She had on a man's shirt, rolled up to her elbows, a pair of jeans that were torn off at the ankle, an old red baseball cap and boys' running shoes. If it hadn't been for the long, black, braided ponytail, she would have thought that this kid was a boy.

Katy walked up to her. She put her hand on the girl's arm. "Are you okay?"

In that instant, it was as if the girl just woke up. She stared into Katy's eyes and put her hand on top of Katy's. "Too late, sorry," she mouthed and pedalled away.

They gaped as she rode down the street wobbling from side to side.

"Weird kid," said Logan, "and she's not very good on that bike, is she?"

"I feel sorry for her," added Ben. "Did you see the way she was dressed?"

"Yeah," agreed Katy, "she looks like she's wearing her dad's clothes." On another level though, somewhere beyond thought, her intuition spoke to her and she felt something strange. *Too late for what?*

Logan gave Ben a nudge forward and linked arms with Katy, "Are we eating or not? Let's go get some food."

CHAPTER 15

"I'VE DECIDED TO BUILD THIS thing—whatever it is," Scott announced to his son. He glanced up from the plans, which were once again spread across the dining room table.

"I'm convinced that this has to be important, or your grandfather never would have hidden it. Besides, I'm intrigued, I have to know what he had in mind. Of course, it would be easier if there was more paperwork somewhere, but who knows, maybe Darth will dig up another tube."

Logan paused. Did his father doubt Logan's story, or was it meant to be a joke?

"We're just lucky we found this." Scott stood up and crossed his arms. He was smiling, "So...what do you say, do you want to give me a hand?"

"Wow! Do you mean it?" Logan was elated. He had always wanted to help his father with a project. He frowned, "But I have something to do tomorrow morning, I'll be home in the afternoon though. Is that okay?" Logan stared nervously at his father. He was afraid the offer might be withdrawn, but he also really needed to find out about that phone call.

"That's okay. I have to make a list of the things we'll need to get started. Then I have to figure out where I can lay my hands on them. I guess you'll still be visiting Darcy in hospital this evening. You probably won't be able to help me for a day or two." Scott waved his finger at Logan, "but after that, I'll be putting you to work!"

Logan smiled. It was something more than watching a hockey game together in silence. Conversation with his dad was always short and sometimes awkward. Here was something different. He went up to his room and called Ben. "Dad's building the machine from the plans, and I get to help!"

Ben answered immediately, "That's great," he said, "but I have to tell you something bad. Darcy's in a coma!"

"What...? How could this happen? Do they know what's wrong with him?" Logan was shocked. "I thought it was a virus. Isn't that what they said?"

"I don't know, but my mom saw him before they moved him into intensive care, and she says she's never seen anything like it. She said she could see all of his veins, like, on his face and his neck and his arms." Ben paused. "We can't go and see him there. My mom says they only allow close family to visit."

"Well, Darcy would want us there!"

"Yeah, I know. Can you call Katy and let her know so she doesn't show up at the hospital?"

"Sure, I'll give her a call, but you know that we have to figure something out. We have to see him somehow."

CHAPTER 16

IT WAS SIX O'CLOCK THE next morning—the sun was already up—when Logan rode into the marina's parking lot. The catwalk was empty. He made his way to Grampa's boat. He cranked the starters and twin Chrysler engines lit up immediately.

As the boat approached the bridge, some anglers above appeared too busy talking to pay him any attention. Logan waved up at them half-heartedly. One of them touched a finger to his ear in a strange way, as if contemplating a wave back. Events of last summer flashed across his mind for some reason, and this made him think that if this were a trap of some kind, no one would know for certain where he was.

He pulled out his phone and sent Ben a text: *Gone to Wolf Island. Need to find out about that call. Home by two o'clock or call my dad.*

The boat glided into the shadows beneath the bridge to the harbour entrance and the lake beyond.

Feeling better, Logan sat back and throttled the big boat up, heading north. For now, he resolved to enjoy the ride.

CHAPTER 17

WOLF ISLAND APPEARED OUT OF the morning fog almost an hour later. It always looked foreboding, but today it felt worse than usual. Not knowing what to expect, this gave him the chills. Logan let the boat drift slowly through the submerged rocks that girded the island. He used a paddle to bring the boat closer to shore before dumping the anchor overboard.

He sat for a moment. Had he made a big mistake by coming here? Ben and Katy thought he was walking into a trap, but Logan found this hard to believe. Grampa had disappeared a year ago. Why would anyone care now? What would they gain by kidnapping or hurting him? Nothing.

Logan rolled up his pant legs as high as he could and took off his boots. He tied the laces together and hung the boots around his neck. He clambered over the side and plunged into the water. It was much deeper and colder than he thought. He clenched his teeth and drew a deep breath.

On shore, he pulled on his boots. The spot where he had landed was knotted with bushes and prickly vines, almost impenetrable. Logan trudged along the beach until he found an opening, an overgrown path.

He stopped and glanced nervously back at the boat—it was his only way home.

Now that he was actually there, he felt his anxiety rising. He needed to shake it off by thinking of something else. Snakes, yes, he remembered what Ed Harris had said about snakes on the island, and mindful of this he was glad he'd replaced his running shoes this morning with hiking boots. While he didn't really believe the story, he didn't want to confirm it either.

It was a warm day, but Logan felt a shiver race up his back as he followed the path from the beach up a hill. The scent of the lake gave way to the sweet smell of poplars and cedar. Half way to the top, the sunlight had burnt through the fog and was now streaming down through the trees. He cupped his hands over his eyes to shield them from the glare. And there, at the top of the hill, a tall, silhouetted figure had stepped directly onto the path in front of him. Logan's mind told him to turn and run, but at the same moment, a big hand gripped his right shoulder from behind. Ben and Katy had been right, and now it was too late to turn back. There was nowhere to run.

CHAPTER 18

THE SMELL OF BACON AND coffee filled the morning air. Ben's mother had just seated herself in one of the shady spots under a maple tree in front of the *Porthole* snack bar. She was holding the table for her husband and son, who had just put in their food orders. This morning it had been her idea to eat out. She wanted a break from the routine, and found herself craving the Porthole's legendary Eggs Benedict.

Inside the restaurant, Ben had just picked up his tray of food. He was carefully making his way through the crowd, when a man in dark glasses stopped him to ask where the washroom was. As Ben held onto his tray with one hand and turned to point out the bathroom with the other, a hand passed over the tray, dropping a tiny amount of dark liquid into his orange juice. Ben never noticed that instead of going to the washroom, the man hesitated only a minute before following him out of the restaurant and walking swiftly away.

"Dad has yours," Ben called as he came up to the table where his mother was seated. "He won't be long."

Just then, someone slammed into him from the side. Ben managed to save everything except the orange juice, which toppled from the tray to the ground, its contents lost to the grass.

"Geez!" Ben yelled as he turned to confront the clumsy girl. "You…"

He stopped short when he realized that this was the very same girl from their earlier encounter in the parking lot. She was dressed in the same clothes, with the same baseball cap pulled down to her eyes.

"Sorry, sorry," she mumbled, holding her hands up, "it was an accident."

"Don't worry about it." Ben's mother had jumped up, out of the way of the flying liquid. She had been frowning, but now she had a sympathetic look. "Don't worry, it's okay, we can always get another one."

"Thank you, sorry, sorry," the girl said in a tiny voice, keeping her head down. She backed away, whirled around and made for her bike.

"Oh dear, she was so embarrassed. Do you know her?" his mother asked, still watching as the girl pedalled away, wobbling as she went.

"No, I think she must be new around here," answered Ben, following his mother's gaze. "I just saw her for the first time yesterday."

"Sorry it took so long. It's a mad house in there," Mr. Kaplan interrupted. He put down his tray of food and turned to take another tray from one of Rod's servers. "I think everyone had the same idea this morning."

He looked at his son's breakfast, untouched, "I honestly thought you'd be finished by now. Have you decided to eat with us for a change? By the way, what did that man want?"

CHAPTER 19

LOGAN WAS TRAPPED. ON THE path above him loomed the tall figure of a man silhouetted against the sun. Behind him, two strong hands now held him firmly in place.

As he started to struggle, Logan caught a glimpse of a man up ahead, now rushing down the path toward him.

"Hey! Stop struggling, everything is okay," said a familiar voice behind him. "Settle down, kiddo."

Logan had no intention of settling down. He ducked and twisted sharply to the side. The hands holding him had lost their grip and he was finally free to run.

"Whoa, stop! It's alright, take it easy!" Ed Harris had his arms out, trying to prevent Logan from bolting.

"Logan, look, it's us. Look at me," his grandfather said. He came up beside them.

"Grampa?" A stunned Logan took a big step backwards. He tripped over his own feet and tumbled into the bushes. The two men standing over him grinned as if sharing a joke.

"It's really us." John McCarthy put his hand out to help his grandson up. "I'm sorry that we scared you."

"Didn't I tell you that we were going to scare the poor kid half to death?" Ed said in a teasing voice.

Back on his feet, Logan threw his arms around both of them. "I - I thought I'd never see you again." He stepped back to look at them, "I don't understand. How did you get here? How did you get away?"

Ed chuckled, "Well, that is a long story. We have a lot to tell you."

"But not now," John interrupted, "it'll have to be later. I'm sorry Logan, but you'll have to wait a little. We need to get out of here. I really need you to come with us. Quickly, we don't want anyone to spot us!" John put his hand on Logan's back and guided him away from the beach.

Ed was still chuckling and shaking his head, "This is going to be fun," he looked down at Logan, "but you'll probably need to see it to believe it."

"Did those aliens do anything to you? Are you sure that you're okay?"

"We're both good, never better," Ed answered. "Come on now, hurry!"

John McCarthy was pushing through tall bushes to make it easier for the others.

Ed started to laugh. "Hey John, I just have to tell him one thing, okay? We'll still keep moving."

Logan's grandfather made a groaning sound, "Oh, for Pete's sake, go ahead, but we can't slow down."

"We won't," Ed assured him. "You know, it's kind of funny really, and you may not believe this, but we never went anywhere, we were never on another planet."

Logan was about to ask something, but Ed held up his hand.

"I know, I know, the last time you saw us was when we were being pulled into that alien lens, so of course it's natural for you to think that we were somewhere out there." Ed rolled his eyes skyward. "But that's not what happened. The truth is, we really were right here. We didn't go anywhere." Ed pointed at the ground. "We've been right here the whole time and the funny part is that we didn't even know it ourselves. I mean, how could we, when everything around us was alien? And it's not like the aliens had a reason to say anything. Why should they when they thought we knew?"

"Aliens? So you were ..."

"Yes, that's right, but it's not what you think," Ed interjected. "It's better for you to see for yourself."

Ed was still chuckling as he dropped back, leaving Logan desperate to know more. But he knew that Ed was teasing him, he'd done this before. Logan would just have to wait until they had reached their destination, wherever that was.

Still, despite Ed's cheerful demeanour, Logan began to think that it would be a good idea to pay more attention to his surroundings. He had landed on the south end of the island, and from the sun, he could tell that they were now walking north, getting more inland as they went. The birches, cedars and poplars surrounded by scrub along the shore gave way to taller maples and oaks. In the dense shade, the air became cooler, shadows deeper. And because the undergrowth was sparser, this made their progress to *wherever they were going* easier.

"You know," Logan was trying to pique their interest so they might tell him more, "everyone thinks that you're on another planet. I mean everyone who was there and saw you being taken away by those aliens. And I don't know if you know this, but the army told everyone that you were killed that day. Even Mom and Dad think that you're dead."

"Humph," John frowned as he briefly glanced back at his grandson.

Logan caught the disapproving look and waited a minute, but there was no comment.

"Where are we going?" he asked. They were still walking north, but there was nothing up that way, Logan knew.

"You'll see, keep going. We'll talk later," said John.

Logan noticed that his grandfather was walking very quickly, even climbing over rocks and dead trees without slowing down. He wasn't even breathing hard. They were higher up now, clear of the shadows of the forest and a soft breeze tugged at their hair. The sky was a brilliant blue.

"How did you know that I would come to the island today? I could have come last night, or waited until tomorrow."

"Ha, that was easy! You wouldn't come in the dark, and we knew you couldn't wait until tomorrow."

"But how did you know that I would come at all?"

"We knew you wouldn't be able to resist that phone call, but just to be sure, we added the symbols. You've always been a curious kid, so we figured all we had to do was make the call and wait."

"Okay, but how did you know that I would land in that spot?"

"Oh, that was easy, too," said John, "We're always monitoring the entire island, as well as the town, and we've been watching you ever since you left the marina."

Now they were climbing a steep hill. The terrain was getting more rocky and harder to climb. "I can't figure out how you could have been here on Earth and not know it." He was puffing a little. "And what about that wormhole that you floated into—it looked like a different planet."

"That's right," Ed said, using tree branches to haul himself forward. "It did, didn't it?"

"Wait until we get inside," John insisted. "We'll answer all your questions then. Come on, we're almost there."

At the top of the hill, Logan saw that they were on the edge of a deep depression. It was bowl-shaped, like a crater. They jogged diagonally down the side, picking up speed as they went. At the bottom, Logan almost plowed into his grandfather's back when John and Ed abruptly halted. They were now standing in the middle of the crater, and all around them was a wall of smooth, rounded, grey rock.

"What are we doing?" asked Logan. "Why are we stopping here?"

John McCarthy turned around to face his grandson, "I want you to remember this spot. Do you think you can do that?"

"Sure," said Logan, affecting a confident air. "The lighthouse is straight over that way across the lake—I saw it from the top of the hill. And the oak tree that you drew on Dad's old treasure map should be over that way, right?"

"Good, he's right!" Ed gave Logan a hearty pat on the back.

John held up his wrist and what looked like a watch. He rotated the bezel and pressed down on the face. Then he held up his hand and pointed it toward the eastern crater wall. Immediately, a faint blue laser light lit up the rock wall in front of them. Logan was astonished to see a portion of the light gray rock begin to darken and reveal a tunnel. Six feet in diameter and perfectly round, it could have been made by a giant drill.

"How did you do that?" Logan couldn't believe what he'd just seen. "What is that thing?" he asked, trying to get a better look at the device on his grandfather's wrist.

"I'll show you later. We have to get inside now, come on!" John waved for him to follow, crouching somewhat as he entered the tunnel. His six-foot four frame was too tall for the opening.

Logan hesitated at the mouth of the tunnel and looked back.

Quickly, before it closes!" Ed reached back and yanked on Logan's arm.

After stumbling forward, a wide-eyed Logan looked back to see nothing but solid rock. The opening had closed without a sound. It was as if it had never been there.

"This is our new home," Ed answered. "This is where we've been since last year when we disappeared."

"Here?" Logan peered into the darkness. "Why didn't you just come home?" he asked, as he continued to follow the two men to where the tunnel ended.

Again, his grandfather held up the instrument on his wrist. A pinpoint of light lit up the wall in front of them, outlining the shape of a door. Without a sound, the door slid upwards into the ceiling revealing a small space, about the size of a bathroom stall. John nudged Logan inside followed by Ed. When the door closed, there was barely room for the three of them to move.

Logan felt that they were moving, but it was impossible to tell in which direction. It took about a minute, but when the door opened, he was astounded to see that they were in a large room, easily three times the size of the gym at school. Directly in front of them on the wall was a scene that Logan couldn't forget. It was the image of an alien landscape, the very one he saw his grandfather and Ed disappear into one year ago.

Logan stared in shock. "Unreal!" Then its significance hit him. "It's just a picture, isn't it? It's not real!" he exclaimed, looking from Ed to his grandfather. "Everyone thought it was real, but it wasn't."

"Nope, but don't feel bad, even we thought it was real until we got here," confirmed Ed, as John chuckled. "There are pictures like this throughout the whole complex. It makes the aliens here feel more at home."

"Aliens? Oh, yeah," Logan said, looking around, as he lowered his voice. "Are they still here? Where are they?"

Out of the corner of his eye, he saw a soft green light approach them. He spun around to find the sphere only a few feet away. He gasped.

It passed behind Logan and hesitated for a second before continuing on to take up a position behind Logan's grandfather.

Logan sensed its power and shivered. It hadn't left the planet either. He found it hard to believe that one year earlier, the sphere was the object of an intense search by a madman and the military, too. All this time, it was beneath their feet.

"You're going to see some amazing things here," John told Logan. "You better hold on to your hat."

CHAPTER 20

Daryl Einhorn was standing on the sidewalk in front of his property. He was trying not to look obvious as he waited for someone, anyone, to pass by.

In his late seventies, he still envisioned himself as quite the lady's man. It was remarkable how he'd suddenly appear whenever a woman would pass in front of his house. He'd dart out and before she knew what was happening, the poor woman was looking for a way to escape. Some of the neighbours wondered if he had cameras monitoring the street. After cornering his victim, he would talk and talk, mainly about himself of course, until the desperate woman came up with an excuse to get away.

Perhaps no one would have minded these annoyances, if it weren't for the fact that he was a really mean gossip. Daryl Einhorn enjoyed the misfortunes of others.

With nobody in sight at the moment, Daryl grabbed the opportunity to scuttle back into his house. His front door was left open for a view of the street, and in moments he was back with a cup of coffee. It was a prop, a drink he slowly nursed as he paced back and forth on his neatly trimmed lawn. He was becoming impatient. He had a particular woman in mind.

A while later, when Brian Littman, the neighbour opposite, arrived home, and before Brian could even exit his car, Daryl was crossing the street, waving his arms, trying to gain Brian's attention.

Brian rolled his eyes and groaned as he closed his car door. *Oh no, so who is it this time?* he wondered. After all, it wasn't as though Brian and Daryl Einhorn were friends, just the opposite was true. Brian knew that it had to be a bit of juicy gossip that Daryl was anxious to share. He'd have to think of an excuse to get away quickly.

"I was just wondering if you'd heard about that boy, Darcy Ryder," Daryl asked, planting himself squarely in Brian's path, "you know, that kid who collapsed right there on my lawn." Daryl was pointing over his shoulder, at the lovely green space of his lawn, where in his mind, a terrible crime against humanity had occurred.

In that brief moment, Brian uttered a silent prayer that he would never retire without a meaningful hobby or pastime. *Kill me now*, he thought.

"Oh, right, I heard about that," Brian said. "It's an awful thing. Have you heard how he is?"

"Oh, I guess you haven't heard the rest," Daryl sighed, doing his best to look concerned. "Poor kid, he's in a coma. And the doctors can't figure out what's wrong with him." Daryl shook his head solemnly, "Really scary thing, the way it came on so fast."

"Yes, I guess so," Brian shook his head, "I sure hope he'll be all right. His parents must be extremely worried." Brian was edging away. Daryl was going to lose him.

"Yes, of course, his poor parents," Daryl added quickly. "I heard that there's another kid in the hospital." He was watching Brian's face with twisted delight. "Katy Prentiss. You might know her father, who is a professor at the university. Apparently, she collapsed in the middle of the night. Her father didn't find her for hours. She was already in a coma by then."

"No kidding? I wonder if there's something nasty going around. I'll have to warn my wife. Thanks for letting me know," Brian said, as he stepped to the side.

Daryl stepped forward. "Katy is a friend of Logan McCarthy, so is Darcy Ryder. They're always hanging around together. I thought at first it was drugs but..."

Brian was looking over his shoulder at his front door, perhaps imagining a rescue by paramedics, a passing Good Samaritan or the Swiss Guard.

"I don't know if you're aware of this, but Cathy and Scott McCarthy just got back from some remote part of Africa. And of all the crazy things," his voice dropped to a conspiratorial whisper, he leaned in towards Brian, "I hear they were examining a cave for alien bones. Weird, don't you think? It's dangerous if you ask me."

Daryl imagined that Brian was interested now. "Anyway, maybe it's crazy," Daryl continued, "but I'm a little worried that they might have brought something back with them, some virus or maybe even a super bug that tagged along with the bones. It's irresponsible. Don't you think?"

"Oh, so they went to Africa this time. I wasn't aware they were back," Brian was now studying the McCarthy house. His eyes narrowed. "Well, whatever this thing is,

I'm sure the doctors will sort it out. And I have to tell you, I don't believe in aliens."

Later that evening, Brian's wife, Marsha Littman, was on the phone with her brother. She was whispering. "Does your daughter, Laura, ever have anything to do with the McCarthy boy, you know, Logan? Because, in case she does, I thought I'd better warn you that a friend of his is sick, and another is in a coma. We heard today that it might have something to do with Scott and Cathy McCarthy's trip to Africa. They were digging in some remote cave, looking for alien bones. God knows what they might have found and brought back with them. Anyway, I thought you might want to warn Laura to stay away from Logan for a while. You know, just to be safe."

CHAPTER 21

FAR BELOW GROUND, WITH THE sphere following close behind, John and Ed led Logan along a series of passageways, descending deeper and deeper into the alien complex. Knowing that it would be impossible to find his way back to that first large room, Logan stayed as close behind the two men as possible. He noticed that the tunnel here was very different from at ground level. The walls were brightly lit somehow.

Something else that grabbed Logan's attention was the floor. It felt soft, like walking on a really thick carpet. He looked down, expecting to find that he was leaving footprints, but there were none. Instead, the floor appeared to be metal, smooth, grey and shiny. He was trying to decide whether it was the floor or the walls, or both, but something was soaking up any sound, making the place eerily quiet. As he happened to glance down again, he caught a glimpse of something, another shadow, something moving around silently behind him. It was probably a trick of the light, but he could identify his grandfather's shadow and the one belonging to Ed, and of course, there was his own. He kept watching, but for sure, there was something else moving, subtly transitioning across his shadow.

Much as he didn't want to, he turned his head to the side, as far as he could, and there, just a few feet behind him, was something, or rather, someone.

"Jeez!" Logan yelped, raising his arms automatically as he jumped back against the wall.

"No, no!" Ed said, grabbing Logan's forearms. "It's okay. We're among friends here."

John didn't want the alien to see Logan's frightened face, so he quickly stepped up beside Ed. "That's right, Logan," he said in a calm voice. "This is one of our new friends."

"I didn't hear him, that's all," Logan blustered, his eyes wide. "He…. just surprised me. Sorry!"

The stranger was standing very still, his head tilted slightly to one side, as if assessing Logan somehow. His large black eyes never blinked.

"This is Teaf," said John, indicating the stranger. "He's Anunnaki."

And there was the sphere. It radiated a soft green light. He recalled that the green colour meant that there was no threat. Even so, it drifted closer to Logan, who returned his gaze to the pale alien, not really grasping his grandfather's words. "Um, Anu-what?"

John continued, "Logan, Teaf is from another world. They call themselves Anunnaki."

"Anunnaki," the name tumbled from Logan's mouth in a meaningless blob.

"I believe we talked about this once. The gods of the ancient *Sumerians*, of ancient Babylon," Ed paused to see if Logan understood, "*where Iraq is now…*"

"Lo...gan." The alien's head was now raised, and his eyes were locked on Logan. His voice was soft, diffused, and seemed to emanate from every direction. "You are not black-headed, either. You are of the Northern race?"

"Yes," John confirmed, "Logan is the one I told you about. He's family, my grandson, he has my DNA. Northern European tribe."

It was a peculiar thing for Grampa to volunteer in the conversation, the significance of which would only dawn on Logan much later. For now, Logan was too tongue-tied to say anything. *Black-headed. What does that mean?* Logan wondered.

The image of the grey aliens of television and movies appeared in Logan's mind. *How did the filmmakers know?*

"Your DNA, yes," was all that Teaf said as he walked ahead and motioned them to follow.

Logan couldn't take his eyes off Teaf as he moved down the passageway. He was at least a foot shorter than Logan and very slightly built. Wiry would have been a better word. Hairless, too. That's what threw Logan: Teaf had no eyelashes and never blinked. He had a gait that was smooth and light, as if gravitation and mechanical joints did not apply. More than anything, it was a sense that he was there but not there, just floating. His appearance was a contradiction: he was imposing, yet ghost-like. Clad in a milky white robe, he wore on his wrist the same device Logan's grandfather wore.

A few more turns and they arrived at what appeared to be their destination, a small rounded doorway. Logan gasped. The room beyond was enormous, with what looked like a fifty-foot-high ceiling and smooth, pastel-coloured walls. The entire length of the room was brightly lit, with neat rows of glass cases or tables filled with plants. A number of aliens were moving about, attending to the plants.

"They grow their own food," Logan mused aloud, "but I figure they'd have to, huh? They couldn't very well go to the grocery store."

"Right," John smiled, "And, yes, they do, but that's in a different area."

"Oh, okay, so what are these plants for?" Logan asked. He could see a few aliens taking a leaf from a plant and putting it into a small glass bottle.

"They're experimenting," said Ed.

"All of this is for research," John added. "These aliens are scientists." He waved his arm around the room. "All of these plants are being tested to see what environment would suit them best. Next, the seeds from these plants are taken to where they have the best chance to survive. That's what the Anunnaki have been doing for hundreds of thousands of years. In fact, almost all of the vegetation here on earth was brought here by them."

Logan thought about this for a moment, having regained his composure. "Even poison ivy?" he joked, because it was everywhere you looked on Wolf Island. John groaned, but Teaf nodded in what appeared to be agreement. Irony was apparently not in the Anunnaki vocabulary.

Logan turned to the alien, but kept his gaze down slightly. "Why do you do it?" Logan asked.

"To preserve life," Teaf answered, tilting his head back to look up at Logan.

Grampa came up to Logan's side and quietly said, "Bow your head and look directly at him when you speak. It's a courtesy."

"Oh, I didn't know, sorry. Do you just save plants?" Logan asked, bowing his head to meet the alien's gaze this time. "Or do you save animals, too?"

"Yes," Teaf said as he turned toward the door.

"All life," Ed elaborated. "If something goes extinct here on earth, say for example the woolly mammoth, you can be sure that there will be more of them somewhere else in the galaxy. So nothing is ever lost."

"Just being here is very exciting," John said. "And just think, there are facilities like this one scattered throughout the galaxy. We're lucky to have one here on Earth."

"They're like the gardeners of the universe," Logan concluded, with some admiration in his voice. He was taking more notice as he looked around and watched the Anunnaki working nearby. They appeared to be absorbed in their work and didn't acknowledge the humans' presence.

"How many—people—are here?" Logan asked his grandfather, sheepishly trying to avoid the *alien* word. "It sure looks like a lot."

"Quite a few, I'm not really sure how many. Look, there's plenty to see, but right now we're going to go somewhere quiet so we can catch up, okay?" John gave Ed a funny look and led Logan further down the corridor.

CHAPTER 22

LOGAN FOLLOWED HIS GRANDFATHER DOWN the hall where John ushered him into a smaller room that was probably a meeting room of some kind. His grandfather stood in the doorway and talked to Ed for a minute. Ed, followed by the sphere, continued along the passageway.

Inside the room, there were a number of odd shaped mounds, likely meant as seats, assembled around what looked like a large mushroom. Two of the seats appeared to be made especially for humans, because they were clearly out of place, the chairs were wider and they were the only ones with backs. Logan was about to sit on one of the smaller, rounder seats when his grandfather gestured toward the chair beside him.

John sat down. A number of aliens entered the room. Logan tensed. They all looked the same to him. He had no idea how or if his grandfather could tell them apart. They all had the same large, black, unblinking eyes—it was impossible to tell where they were looking. They had the same pale white skin, and less prominent mouths and noses, too. Logan watched them taking their seats, sitting poker straight. They were turning and tilting their heads, gazing around the room, as though they were in the middle of a conversation.

Being in this surreal place with no natural light and surrounded by all these strange beings, Logan could see how Ed and his grandfather had concluded that they must have been on another planet or indeed on a spaceship.

Amid this strange milieu, his thoughts turned to Ben. How could he explain all this to his friend? It was going to be a lot for him to take in. Not only did Logan have to tell Ben that his grandfather and Ed Harris were alive and well, but where they had been for the last year and with whom.

John cleared his throat and leaned forward, getting everyone's attention. "Yes, of course," he nodded, "he needs to know." He turned his chair to face Logan. "I know about Darcy," he said in a hushed voice, "and we know he's been poisoned."

Logan couldn't believe what he'd just heard. "No!" he said, shaking his head. "No, he can't have been. The doctor says he's just got a bad virus."

All the aliens in the room turned toward Logan. He realized that they sympathized, and he could actually feel it, in his heart and in his mind.

"I can't tell you how sorry I am about Darcy," began John, "but you have to listen to me, because I need you to explain to your father what's going on. I require his help and your help as well. The situation is grave, but before I get into it, can you please explain to me what your father thinks happened to Ed and me? Before you say anything, there is something I need to warn you about." John closed his eyes for a moment before leaning forward. "The sphere must not know what's going on. Do you understand? When you're in the sphere's presence, I don't want you to say anything about this situation, and try not to get excited or nervous. We know from a year ago that the sphere can sense things. The trouble is, if it decides to do something about this threat, the outcome might be worse than anything coming at us from outer space. We don't want it to solve one problem by creating a bigger one. Is that clear?"

"I understand," Logan nodded. "I'll be careful, I promise."

"I know you will," John nodded gravely. "And now I need to know everything the army told your father. Does he really believe that we're dead?"

Logan stared at his grandfather for a brief moment. He was overwhelmed but at the same time relieved. Now was the time for the entire truth to come out. It would take a huge burden off his shoulders.

Logan related the story. "When Mom and Dad got home from South America, two men came to the house. One was a man from the power company and the other was someone from the police department. They said they were there to explain what caused the fire and collapse of the old power plant. The accident was entirely the fault of one insane man, they said. They even suggested that we should sue Globicon."

He rolled his eyes and continued, "A day later, they called it a national security issue, and the army brought in a bunch of men to search every inch of your house and Ed's house, even the barn. They left plenty of holes in the ground around both of your properties, and Dad insisted that they had to fill them in when they were done. I was there when the Globicon guys and then the army carted away the files from your office and trashed the place."

"I'm really sorry, Grampa," Logan said. "But the army told Ben, Katy and I that something terrible would happen to our families if we told anyone the real truth. We knew they were following us, and we were scared, so we didn't."

By the end, John was leaning back in his chair, his eyes were closed and he was frowning.

"So... they've convinced your father that I'm dead," John said, opening his eyes, frowning. "Well, I guess I'm not surprised, they can be pretty damn convincing. And don't you worry, son, anyone would have been afraid in that situation."

"The army used DNA," Logan blurted, sitting up straighter. He had just remembered his grandfather's strange remark earlier. "That's how they convinced Mom and Dad that you were really dead."

Ed came into the room. "Hah," he made a face as he grumbled, "DNA, eh, that would make it sound real."

"Yes, it does," agreed John. "It's what we expected. I don't suppose they wanted any inconvenient questions."

"They even threatened Katy's father. I think he must be pretty scared too, because he's never said a word about it, even to Katy."

"That doesn't surprise me either. Heaven only knows what they threatened him with. These people will protect their secrets at any cost," John was shaking his head. "The thing is that we don't have time to worry about them for now. There's a much bigger problem to deal with."

John and Ed stopped talking for a moment. They were staring at one alien in particular seated near the door.

A moment later John turned back to Logan, "Okay, here it is. As you know, when I found the sphere, it was aboard a space ship that had crashed ages ago in the Arctic. From the bones I found, I had guessed that the crash happened when the North Pole was warm and tropical. The feeling I had from the sphere, and still have, is that the sphere had once belonged to an ancient race of aliens, probably far older than the ones who had it on the ship. I think that the aliens from the ship had either found the sphere and were taking it back to their home world like a prize, or they had stolen it. You saw the video I recorded, didn't you, and the ship, and how I found the sphere?"

"Yes," nodded Logan, "the professor showed me."

"Good, well, the aliens from the ship have come back," John explained, "and now they want us to give them the sphere."

"But if they're going to poison people, why don't we just give it to them?" Logan asked.

John and Ed glanced at each other. "We're hoping it never comes to that. These aliens are called the 'Cioth' and they are the most warlike race in the galaxy. They're cruel and devoid of compassion—they delight in the pain and suffering of others."

"You must understand," added Ed, "that if they get the sphere, there will be nothing stopping them from destroying the earth."

CHAPTER 23

BEN TORE INTO THE MARINA parking lot, standing on the pedals all the way. He jumped off his bike without stopping and ran to the catwalk, while his bike crashed into the hedge. He paused though and returned to the pop machine—it was warm that day and he needed a drink. With just enough money in his pocket, he got what he wanted and headed for Logan's grandfather's boat. The slip was in a prime location, and from there he had a commanding view of anything coming into the harbour. He sat, dangling his feet over the water while he sipped his pop and waited.

After barely two minutes, a stranger approached him from further along the catwalk. The man was wearing dark glasses and his hands were shoved deep into his pockets. Ben's head started to buzz, so he gave the stranger a cautious once over and looked around for any other source of danger or trouble.

In the next slip, two men were standing beside a boat, talking in low voices. As they glanced sideways at Ben and the stranger, he grew fearful.

"Excuse me, could you help me, please?" the man asked politely. "I've lost my phone, and I need to make an important call."

"Oh, okay," said Ben, as he continued to keep an eye on the two men. "Um, I have a cell phone," he said, as he stood up and began digging through his pockets.

"No, no," interrupted the man, "I won't use your phone, it will be a long call, I just need to find a telephone booth."

"Oh, well, uh…there's a phone booth at the corner of the parking lot." Ben was starting to rub his forehead. The buzzing was getting worse.

"I didn't see one," the man said, shaking his head.

"Yeah, it's hard to see. Let me show you," said Ben, leading the way. He hoped the buzzing would stop if he left the catwalk. "I think the bushes have grown up around it, and that's probably why you missed it." Ben was trying not to show how much pain he was in, but the buzzing was increasing in intensity.

As the stranger followed Ben along the catwalk, another man approached the slip from the opposite direction. He bore a striking similarity to the first man. He pulled a small vial from his pocket and crouched down before emptying a few drops of dark liquid into Ben's drink.

At the edge of the parking lot, Ben pointed out where the booth was located. He turned to retrace his steps but glanced back to see if the man was making his call. The booth was empty. The man was gone, and there was no one around. *Strange*, Ben thought, *where could he have gone?* Confused, he returned to the boathouse.

The buzzing still hurt, but somewhat less. It was a relief to see that the two men had left. He sat down at the edge of the slip and leaned forward enough to check out his reflection. Even when his head hurt like crazy, he looked the same. No one would ever guess what was going on in his head. For some reason this surprised him. At the very least, his hair should be standing on end.

For what seemed like the hundredth time, he checked his watch. Logan was running out of time and Ben was getting more and more anxious. Absently he reached for his drink, just as someone approached him from behind. Before he knew what was happening, he was shoved off the catwalk.

He plunged face first into the murky, green water. It was stagnant and reeked of gasoline and dead fish.

"What the hell!" Ben yelled as he swam the few feet to the catwalk, where it took all of his strength to pull himself up and out of the water. He leapt to his feet, and glanced around.

In the distance he spotted someone running toward the parking lot. He rubbed his eyes and focussed. It was the strange girl in the funny clothes. She glanced back with a nervous look. "You'd better run!" he yelled after her. "Good thing you have a head start."

Ben scowled. He watched her disappear. *There must be something wrong with her*, he thought to himself. *That's the second time that she knocked into me.*

He frowned at his can of soda, now floating in the water, but to his surprise, the buzzing in his head had stopped. *Maybe she was the cause.*

I'm going to get you, he thought as he looked down at his wet clothes and running shoes still filled with water.

CHAPTER 24

It was twenty minutes past two, and still no Logan. Twice, Ben had gotten up to leave, but changed his mind. He would give Logan ten more minutes.

His clothes were sticking to him, and he smelled as if he'd been cleaning fish, but the worst thing was the way the water was squishing in his shoes. Not entirely sure that that crazy girl had left, Ben sat farther back from the water, facing the parking lot.

The familiar idle of Logan's speedboat caused Ben to whirl in that direction. Relieved, he rose to wave to his friend.

"Hey, Ben," Logan called, "you gotta' hear this!" Then, as though he'd had second thoughts, he scowled and didn't say another word until he'd docked the boat. He looked around and lowered his voice, "You won't believe it."

Ben was full of questions. "What do you mean? Did you find out who called you? Was there someone over there? Was it the army? Because I wouldn't believe anything they say. You know, they're…"

"No, no, it wasn't the army!" Logan interrupted and shook his head. He jumped out of the boat and grabbed Ben by the arm, putting his finger to his lips. "Come on, let's talk in the parking lot," he said, urging his sodden friend along the catwalk. "Um, what happened to you?"

"I have something to tell you, too," Ben said over his shoulder. His shoes squished as they went.

They'd barely made it to the parking lot, when Logan said, "Yeah, okay, but me first. It was my grandfather and Ed! That's who called me and put those symbols on my phone. They've been here the whole time. When we thought they were on another planet, they weren't. They were right there on Wolf Island!"

Logan's arms were moving about as he talked in a loud whisper. "They have been living with aliens. Can you imagine? There's a huge complex, it's under the island, that's where the aliens live. They're good ones though, and smart," Logan assured Ben. "They save animals and plants from extinction. They've been doing it for thousands of years. On the way back, I was thinking, when we were fishing over there, they were hundreds of feet below us the whole time." Logan had not stopped to take a breath.

Ben stared back. He didn't know what to say.

"I'm not crazy Ben, it's the truth, honest. The next time I go, you can come with me, you'll see. Right now, we have to go to my house. Grampa wants me to tell Dad that he and Ed are still alive. He needs my dad to help them. See, I know why Darcy got sick, it's because these other aliens want the sphere. They're really bad and they are going to keep poisoning people until my grandfather gives them the sphere."

Logan grabbed Ben by the arm and began to jog toward the bicycle rack when Ben finally spoke, "Katy, too."

Logan came to a halt, as soon as he heard her name. "What do you mean, *Katy too*?"

"She's in the hospital," Ben's voice trailed off.

"When did this happen"? Logan demanded.

"Her dad found her on the floor in the bathroom this morning," Ben explained. "He called an ambulance right away. She's in the hospital."

"Is she okay?" Logan was stunned.

Ben shook his head. "Katy has the same thing as Darcy. She was in a coma when her dad found her. He called my mom and your dad. He's pretty upset. Anyway, he wanted us to know. I'm going over to see her and Darcy tonight."

Logan looked around for a moment. His hands were clenched. "We have to do something." His tone was urgent. "Come on, I've got to talk to my dad."

Minutes later, the pair swung into Logan's driveway and hopped off their bikes.

"Logan!" someone nearby called.

Mr. Einhorn was scurrying across the lawn toward them. Both boys continued walking, trying to pretend they hadn't heard him. They needed to get inside. He was the last person they wanted to see.

"Wait! Wait a minute!" he yelled.

Logan stopped and turned, without saying a word. He stared at his neighbour.

"I hear your friends are sick," Einhorn said, as he came to halt in front of the boys. "I just wanted to say how sorry I am to hear it. Do you know how they are?"

"I haven't seen them yet today," answered Logan.

"Oh, well, I was just wondering, because my wife, Ivy, was talking to her friend, who's a nurse at the hospital and she says that the young girl—Katy, is it? —is in a coma now." Einhorn wore a thin, insincere smile. "Umm, by the way, Logan, you know, ha, ha, just a little curious actually, if your parents happened to bring anything back with them from their dig, you know, anything interesting?"

Logan's face fell. He knew instantly what Einhorn was implying. Ben dragged Logan by the arm and led him toward the front door. He looked back over his shoulder and gave the neighbour a scathing look.

"Did they?" Einhorn called after them. "Has Katy Prentiss been to your house recently?"

"Go away, we're in a hurry." Ben's face was flushed as he pushed Logan forward. "That man is a real jerk, just ignore him. You have to go and talk to your dad."

CHAPTER 25

Scott McCarthy was on the phone in his office when the boys stepped into the hallway. "Come on, Ted, really? You can't get it any sooner? This is a special project I'm working on. I'd really appreciate a favour."

The boys took off their jackets and waited impatiently in the hall. Logan had started to pace, he was angry.

"Great! I can't tell you how much I appreciate this, Ted," Scott sounded pleased, "I'll pick it up myself tomorrow afternoon… Right… See you soon."

He got up from his desk and came out into the hall to find two long faces. "What's up boys? Is everything okay, are you feeling all right?"

Logan's head was down, "Katy is in the hospital. I just heard that she's in a coma like Darcy."

"Oh, yes, I know, it's just terrible, I'm really sorry Logan. Her father called here today. He was beside himself with worry. I think we should all go over to the hospital after dinner. Maybe we can give a little support, and at least keep the professor company." Scott's voice was sympathetic.

"Yeah, I want to, Dad, but right now, I need to talk to you, it's an emergency," Logan gave his father an intense stare.

"Oh," Scott nodded, "I have to make a phone call, but it can wait a few minutes. What…"

Logan spun around. "Where's Mom?" he asked, "I have to tell her, too."

* * *

"Okay," Logan began, as he stared down at the table, his hands pressed between his knees, "…you may not believe this at first," he glanced up at his father, and began to talk very fast, "but Grampa is still alive. The army made up a story because of what really happened. But it's all a big lie. They blew the roof off the old power plant to cover it up."

Ben never looked up, but he nodded in agreement. After a moment, he got up and retreated to the hall. He couldn't do anything to help Logan and he wanted out of the line of fire.

Scott folded his arms and shook his head, while he gave his son a hard stare. "What in the hell are you talking about?" he asked. "You know that your grandfather died. They proved it. It was your grandfather's DNA. This isn't funny, son."

Logan held up his hand. "Wait, wait," he exclaimed, "Grampa thought you might say that, so I'll prove it!" He jammed his hand into his pocket and pulled out a tiny cube. He sat it on the table in front of his father and leaned back, arms folded.

"What is this thing?" Scott was upset.

"Grampa made this to give to you."

Scott looked skeptical as he leaned over to get a closer look. In a moment, his father's face was projected above the cube. John McCarthy's voice could be heard. "Son, I know this will be a shock, but I am alive and I need your help."

Scott's face changed from anger to astonishment to confusion. "How can this be real?"

"He said you might need proof!" Logan asssderted. His hands were trembling.

Logan's mother dropped into the chair beside her husband. She wore a shocked expression as she watched the message from her father-in-law. When it finished, she stared at her son for a moment. "I don't understand any of this. How is this possible?" She was pointing at the cube. "And why would the army lie? What a cruel thing to do! More importantly, why would *you* lie about this?" she blurted out, eyeing Logan fiercely.

"I know, I'm sorry," Logan conceded. "The government didn't want you or anyone else to know the truth, about what really happened."

"What does he say?" Ben said, craning his neck around the doorway.

Logan stared at his friend for a moment before turning to his parents, "Is it okay if Ben sees it? He already knows what really happened. He was there the whole time," Logan explained. "He saw Grampa disappear."

"So *now* you're asking for permission?" his exasperated mother replied.

Scott studied Ben's anxious face before deciding. "Okay, what the hell! He picked up the cube and held it up for Ben.

The message was simple: *Scott, please believe Logan's account of what happened last summer. The army is covering up the truth. Please come to the island as soon as you can, I need your help.*

"That's true!" Ben was nodding vigorously, "First the army covered it up, then they threatened us to shut us up. They said that they'd hurt our families and we believed them."

Scott was staring at the cube. His face was red, chin out. A vein pulsed in his forehead. He didn't appear to have heard Ben. "Later, we'll have to have a long talk about why, this whole time, you didn't tell me that my father was still alive." Logan had never seen his father this angry.

Logan and Ben dropped their heads again. They were too ashamed to look Scott in the eye.

After staring at their bowed heads for a minute or two, Scott got up slowly and leaned against the kitchen island, his arms crossed. "Okay you two, start talking. I want to hear the entire story, from your perspective. Don't leave anything out," he demanded.

It took almost two hours to tell Logan's father about everything that had happened the previous year. The boys took turns, interrupting each other trying to get it all out.

"And you saw my father today, that's where you went this morning, and he's okay?" Scott asked.

"Yes, he's fine," confirmed Logan. "So, he and Ed have been on, I mean, under, Wolf Island, for a year."

Ben was squirming in his seat, dying to ask a question.

"I guess he knows that I thought he was dead." Scott stared at Logan, who nodded back. "Does he know I have his plans?" Scott jerked his thumb toward the dining room.

"No," Logan said, rolling his eyes, "I forgot to tell him."

"And this is the first time anyone knew of this alien facility?" Scott was struggling to process the news.

"Yes, sir," answered Logan.

"And you saw real aliens over there?" interrupted Ben, his eyes bright.

Logan smiled and nodded back at him, "Not the bad ones, these were the good ones. Grampa calls them the Anunnaki."

"Wait a minute," Scott held up his hand. "I want to see if I've got this straight. These aliens who first found the sphere were transporting it back to their planet. They crashed on Earth, several thousands of years ago, and my dad found it. Is that right?"

"Professor Prentiss says it's more like millions, but yeah," Logan nodded.

Cathy tried to interject, "It sounds to me to be far too old for these aliens to have owned it. Civilizations don't last that long. The sphere is far too ancient to be…"

"So, they might have thought it was lost forever," Scott interrupted, "until they heard something while monitoring communications here on Earth, correct? And that's how they found out it was here?"

"That's right, probably because of Globicon, and now those aliens want it back," Logan explained, "but Grampa says the sphere has bonded with him, it would never leave him behind. So, if the aliens take the sphere, they would have to take Grampa, too."

"Well, that's not going to happen!" Scott said plainly.

Cathy had been quiet for a while, doing a slow burn. "It's called imprinting," Cathy sighed. "The strong bond that formed between the sphere and John, it's called imprinting!"

Everyone paused, confused by her outburst.

Cathy was exasperated. "Perhaps if you listened to me occasionally...?" She shrugged before continuing. "The sphere has to be part machine, part organic—a sentient—a thinking being. Think about it. For all we know, it was alone in that wrecked spaceship for millions of years, alone without any company. Then along came John McCarthy after all that time, and the sphere bonded with him. Like a child to a parent. It trusts him. But don't listen to me: I'm just a forensic anthropologist!"

"Sorry, just caught up in the moment," Scott's face burned red. He paused before looking at Logan. "And so, now you're saying that these aliens who," Scott cast a conciliatory glance at Cathy, "*claim* to own the sphere are going around poisoning the people that your grandfather knows, so he'll give this sphere thing back to them. Is that right?" Scott finished.

"That's right," agreed Logan. "And the aliens under Wolf Island, the Anunnaki, are trying to find a cure for the poison. Grampa says that the Anunnaki won't interfere with anything that happens on Earth. It's some kind of rule or something... unless it threatens the balance of life."

"These Anunnaki must be afraid of the Cioth, the Cioth must be more advanced," reasoned Scott.

"No! They're not. It's the other way around!" Logan exclaimed. "The Anunnaki are more advanced than the Cioth. It's the Cioth who are the ones who are afraid, that's why they're drugging people, but not actually killing anyone. Darcy and Katy could stay in a coma forever, but they won't die, because that would upset the balance of life."

"But they'll eventually starve to death if they don't get medical care," concluded Cathy."

"The Anunnaki have been here on Earth for thousands of years. Grampa says they've grown to like humans a little. They also know that the Cioth are a violent and cruel species, and that's why they're trying to find a cure for the poison. Besides, the sphere is unbelievably powerful, it shouldn't be in the hands of the Cioth. Grampa says that if no cure is found, and the Cioth don't get the sphere, they could poison everyone on the planet."

"Sounds like guerrilla warfare, terrorism" Cathy mused. "Not enough for the Anunnaki to become fully involved, but enough to compel us to surrender the sphere to the Cioth. Very cunning."

Scott nodded. "I'll talk to my father. Maybe he has an idea. We'll see him tomorrow. Right Logan?"

"Yes!" Logan nodded. "He wants us to come, he's really anxious to see you. He said to try and get to Wolf Island before sunrise, tomorrow morning."

"All right, let's do that," said Scott.

"Can I come, too?" Ben begged, "I've been around since the beginning."

"Sure, I guess so," Scott replied.

Cathy climbed onto a bar stool and watched her husband's expression. It wasn't difficult to know what was on his mind. He was thinking about the reunion tomorrow with his father and Ed Harris. That was wonderful news. Still there was a question that was nagging her, a question that at some point she wanted the answer to. That spaceship, the one that crashed, what happened to it, was it still there?

CHAPTER 26

Decades ago in the Canadian arctic, the expedition was over. A military transport aircraft headed south with John McCarthy and his team aboard. John sat apart from the others with a rather large box in his lap. Despite repeated requests to stow the box, John refused and the loadmaster relented.

"Scientists!" the loadmaster was heard muttering under his breath.

Well beyond the horizon to the north, a large contingent of Russian Naval Infantry marines closed in on the source of a giant electromagnetic pulse that had flattened half of the world's electrical grids. The Russians were well into Canadian territory and were *not* there to measure the effects of climate change. It was several days travel, and the tracked vehicles, painted in arctic camouflage, were well matched to the terrain and time of year.

The marines pored over the wreckage of an alien spacecraft, long dead. Despite its alien construction, Russian scientists had concluded that the power source had been removed. When this happened, they could not say for certain. The release of the pulse suggested it had been very recently taken. It was a reasonable assumption.

Still, even without the power source, the ship was regarded as a prize worth stealing. Why others had not claimed it was a mystery.

* * *

A few days later an Arctic Ranger on patrol radioed his superiors that he'd seen some strange marks on the ground, evidence of a huge excavation and tracked vehicles, perhaps they were tanks or armoured personnel carriers, he couldn't say, arriving from the north and departing in the very same direction. He'd never seen anything like it. One set of armoured vehicle tracks was very deep indeed, which told him that whatever was excavated was probably taken with them. In other words, a giant hole in the snow and tracks in the snow. You might as well have said, *this way to Russia*.

He would follow these tracks north for some two days. It was noon when he came upon a scene of total devastation. In the snow, bits of steel, completely shattered into tiny bits, glittered under the wan northern sun. There was no trace of life, no blood anywhere. An oddity did catch his eye though, something well beyond the blast radius: a Super 8 millimeter camera. It appeared to have been thrown clear.

The Ranger was familiar with this type of camera. He'd seen them used for filming Arctic documentaries. It was badly charred, but in any case, he knew that the film had to be developed in a lab to be viewed. What it had recorded were three bright lights on the horizon, closing at immense speed.

Before he could make his second report, and in a bit of very bad luck, a polar bear swatted the Ranger from behind. The camera went flying into the air and the Ranger was taken, never to be seen again.

Later in the week, an overflight by a patrol aircraft revealed nothing of any consequence at the reported location, and the matter of the missing Ranger was quietly dropped.

CHAPTER 27

THE TRIP TO THE HOSPITAL that evening left Ben and Logan feeling helpless and demoralized. Both of their friends were still in a coma—there had been no change. Worse still, since Logan and Ben were not family, they weren't allowed into the intensive care unit.

Ben's father appeared. "There's no change I'm afraid," he said. He handed his son some money and suggested that the boys go out for pizza and meet them at home later.

"I really hate this," Logan grumbled. "I want to tell them that their kids aren't going to die. They're just going to stay asleep until the Anunnaki can find a cure."

"Whenever that is," Ben grumbled back.

"What really scares me is what if the Cioth gave Darcy or Katy too much poison? What if they really could die?"

Ben shook his head. "Don't even say that."

"And the hospital won't even let us see them!" Logan added. "If you ask me, that's just stupid, because who knows them better than us? We're their best friends, and that's as good as family is, isn't it?" Logan kept turning around and glaring back at the hospital.

"Yeah, it is, but it might not matter, not if the Anunnaki are as smart as you think. Because if they are, it probably won't be long before they find a cure. Don't you think?" Ben sounded optimistic.

"I hope so," said Logan, as he kicked at something on the ground, "but Grampa warned me that it might take a miracle, because the poison was made on the Cioth planet, and that's a place that nobody knows anything about."

Logan stopped talking when a number of people caught up with them. The few that passed by appeared to be hospital staff and visitors heading home. After last year though, the boys had learned to be cautious. They would say nothing until they were finally alone.

This suited Logan, who was thinking about his mother's words from earlier. "How could an inferior race such as the Cioth obtain such a powerful device in the first place, millions of years ago? Were they capable of building such a thing, it didn't sound like it." She was convinced that the sphere was probably much older than anyone realized. It probably existed before there even was a Cioth species. So, where did the sphere come from, and what was its purpose?

The sun was just setting, and lights were turning on here and there along the street. Ben broke the silence, "Did any of the other aliens talk to you or just that one. I was just curious about how they communicate. Was it telepathy? Are they vegetarians? It sounds like they might be since they grow their own food. How many do you think live there?"

Logan answered all of Ben's questions the best he could, until at last they arrived at the pizza place. They expected it to be busy, and they were right, it was packed with people coming from the movie theatre up the street. The boys placed their orders and went to sit outside on the patio near the sidewalk.

Almost immediately, Ben's head started to buzz. It was just mildly irritating, but he began to look around, trying to determine the source of the threat. In no time, the warning became more forceful, painful. Ben propped his arm on the table, and rested his head in his hand.

A few minutes later, a girl in a red apron delivered the pizza and drinks to their table. Logan knew the girl's brother, so they talked for a few minutes.

Ben was preoccupied with searching the faces surrounding them. For all his vigilance, he didn't see the man in dark glasses watching them from inside the restaurant, but moments later, he began to feel better, the buzzing had decreased and he felt calm again.

"I didn't realize how hungry I was." Logan said, shovelling in a big bite.

Ben was poking straws into their drinks, when, behind them, someone screamed. It sounded like a girl. When the boys turned in their seats, they were surprised to see that same girl, the strange one from the marina. She was trying to hold on to the handlebars of her bike, while Danny and Wayne, the town's notorious bullies, were pushing her back and forth between them and laughing.

"Did you find those clothes at the dump?" Wayne taunted.

"Yeah! I guess that makes you dumpster girl, right?" Danny joined in. "I like that. Dumpster girl!"

Logan jumped up from his seat and yelled, "Hey, leave her alone!" He started to march in their direction.

"Losers!" Ben shouted, "So now you're picking on girls?" He was following close behind Logan as he watched Danny snatch the girl's hat off her head and throw it into the air. Wayne had grabbed the back of her shirt and was about to pull her off her bike when Logan yelled again.

"Why don't you pick on someone your own size?" Logan was getting closer.

"Cowards!" Ben yelled as loud as he could. "You only pick on someone smaller!"

Danny and Wayne stopped and turned around. They stood still for a moment. Danny smiled as he leaned over to say something to Wayne. The pair pushed off on their bikes, barrelling toward Ben and Logan, forcing them to jump out of the way. The pair whizzed past, and skidded up to Ben and Logan's table to grab their drinks.

"Suckers!" the bullies yelled. They raced down the street drinks in hand, laughing as they went.

"Nice, really nice," Logan muttered angrily. "They took our drinks!"

Ben no longer cared about Danny or Wayne. He just wanted to talk to the girl. He wanted to ask her why she kept knocking into him. Was it on purpose? But he'd missed her again. She was already pedalling as fast as she could in the opposite direction.

Logan rested his arm on Ben's shoulder. He was smiling. "Did you see her face? She's kind of pretty without that stupid hat on. And look at her go. She can ride pretty well now, can't she?"

CHAPTER 28

LOGAN'S EYES FLICKED OPEN AT four in the morning. This should have been far too early, but for many reasons he was anxious to start the day. He dressed in seconds, grabbed his backpack and ran down the stairs. From the hallway, Logan could hear the radio in the kitchen. It was reporting six new cases of the terrible new virus.

"Eight young people are now in a coma", the radio announcer said. "It's been reported that all of the new cases had one location in common. The health department is investigating. Doctors are reminding people to cover their faces when sneezing and everyone must remember to wash their hands thoroughly and regularly. Stay indoors. Practise social distancing."

His parents were staring at the radio, listening intently to the news.

"Did I hear you on the telephone last night, mom?" Logan interrupted. "I thought I heard you say something about Danny and Wayne.

"Yes, you did," his mother confirmed. "The story was about them," she said pointing toward the radio. "They were taken to the hospital last night. I guess they're just two of the latest victims."

"But Ben and I saw them last night, at the pizza parlour. They were okay then."

"Is that right?" his father asked. "Because that would've been just an hour or two before they got sick. Sounds to me like you and Ben were lucky. Did you happen to see anyone strange around?"

"No," said Logan, "nothing out of the ordinary."

"I see. Well, I've made up my mind," his father said firmly. "From now on we don't eat out anymore." He turned to Logan, "Just food from home."

"Right," answered Logan.

"We know who's doing this, but we don't know if it's actually contagious, do we?" Cathy looked nervous.

"They took our drinks," Logan interjected, at last making the connection.

"Who took your drinks?" asked Cathy.

"Danny and Wayne, they stole our drinks."

Scott's eyebrows furrowed. "So, your grandfather was right, the aliens are targeting the people closest to him. I'll bet the poison that Katy, Danny and Wayne got was probably meant for you."

"No, that's not right. I know Grampa thinks that, but how could they know about me?" Logan sounded skeptical.

"Well, if you think about it, they are more advanced than we are. They probably have the technology to track the sphere, which probably led them to Milford."

Cathy was standing near the table, holding two lunch bags. Her hands trembled. "It's terrible the way they're putting people to sleep with a poison. Did you hear what the radio is calling it? The Big Sleep. I've heard Sleeping Beauty, too. They say that a disease specialist is being called in." She pushed the bags toward her son. "Here, in case you get hungry, and you should probably grab a few bottles of water as well. Please remember to call me when you can. I really need the two of you to be careful, okay?"

Logan could see how worried and upset his mother was. "We're just going to see Grampa, and the aliens grow tons of food over there. We'll be fine, honest."

"Listen, will you both remember to tell John and Ed how relieved and happy we are that they're alive and well; and how much they were missed, of course."

"We will," promised Logan.

"Are you still going to pick that part up from Ted?" Scott asked Cathy. "If you go, please come straight home afterward. On second thought, I can just courier it."

"Scott, I'm going. I don't want to be stuck in the house all day. I'll just keep my distance from people as much as I can."

Scott just nodded. He knew that there was no arguing with Cathy, and maybe she'd be safer out of the house and away from Milford. The good thing was, as long as she kept busy, perhaps she wouldn't worry as much. He didn't want to say that aloud though.

Out in the hall, Scott checked that the plans were still in the fishing rod case. He strapped the case securely to his backpack and pulled it on. Logan stashed two bottles of water and the lunch bags into his own backpack, and waited by the front door.

"Okay, we're off," Scott said. "If we're going to be longer than we thought, I promise we'll call." He hugged his wife a little longer than usual and kissed her goodbye before opening the door and heading down the walk.

Logan whispered to his mother as she hugged him, "Don't worry, mom, Grampa won't let anything happen to us. He'll be watching the whole time."

As he headed for the car, Logan noticed their neighbour marching back and forth on his front lawn. It was not even dawn, and he was cutting the grass, while staring at them as they got into the car and backed out of the driveway.

"Isn't it a weird time to be cutting the lawn?" Logan murmured. "The sun isn't even up yet."

"That's for sure," agreed his father, "definitely weird, but at least it isn't pouring rain this time."

Later, Logan checked his watch as they pulled into the marina parking lot. It was ten minutes to five. After a quick calculation, he figured that by the time they got the boat ready and sailed to the island, they would arrive pretty much when they said they would.

As the two walked across the parking lot, they weren't surprised to find Ben leaning against the soda pop machine.

CHAPTER 29

THE SUN WAS JUST PEEKING over the hills and that made it difficult to see. Logan glanced back from the passenger seat to find Ben fast asleep. He didn't wake up until Logan called out. "There! Over there, Dad, that's the place." Logan had spotted his landing spot from last time. "I told Grampa we'd try to land there."

When Scott answered, "Right," it was the first word he'd uttered since he'd gotten into the boat. He was thinking about seeing his dad, after all this time believing that he was dead. He just wished it were under better circumstances.

Scott scanned the beach as the boat drifted slowly toward shore. The boys each grabbed a paddle to keep the boat away from the rocks until they were about fifteen feet from shore, where they dropped the anchor.

On the beach, Logan led the way, while Ben and Scott followed behind. Logan made it to the top of the hill, where his grandfather and Ed emerged from the brush.

Father and son hugged, even pulling Ed in. There were a few tears, laughter, and pats on the back. Scott stood back and glared at his father.

"Why didn't you let me know that you were alive?" he asked in a raw voice. "Do you know how horrible it was to come home and find the police on my doorstep, telling me that you were dead? That you'd been crushed to death when the power plant roof collapsed?"

"Look, I'm really sorry, you have to forgive me," John began. "When you got back from South America last year, I really thought that I was on an alien planet. Ed and I had no idea that we were under the island in an alien lab! How could we? By the way, the reason the aliens didn't tell us our location was because they thought we already knew! You have to understand, Scott, these aliens didn't invite us to drop in on them—that was the sphere's doing. It evaluated the situation on the surface and decided that we were in trouble. It could sense that I didn't want to be taken by the army, so it opened a worm hole to the Anunnaki facility, beneath the island."

"You could have called!"

"It was six months before we knew where we were. And you must know, when you're several hundred feet below the surface, the reception is terrible! I did want to call, but that would have meant doing it from the surface, and that meant the army might pick it up. I did try to call Logan when I first got here, but I doubt he heard it." Scott shot a withering glance at Logan.

The conversation went back and forth, until they found themselves atop the hill, overlooking the crater. Scott stopped talking long enough look around. "Where are we?" he asked. "There's nothing here."

John grinned at his son, "Follow me, Scott. You're going to love this." He led the group to the bottom of the depression, where he held up his wrist and in line with the rocky slope.

"What are you …?" Scott stopped as his eyes opened wide. The rock wall dissolved into a dark entrance.

"Cool, this is so amazing! What is that thing?" Ben was staring at the watch on John's wrist. However, before John could answer, Ben was already surging forward. "Where does the tunnel go? Are we going inside?" He just couldn't believe it.

Logan watched in awe as his friend stepped through the entrance without hesitation. He showed no sign of fear.

They eventually caught up to Ben at the end of the tunnel where the odd little elevator was hidden. Ben was peering around and knocking on walls, trying to figure out what to do next.

"Calm down," John ordered, holding his hand up. "From here on, stop running, and stay with us!" Ben clenched his hands and nodded.

CHAPTER 30

Ben gaped when the elevator door slid open to reveal a large well-lit room. In front of them was the same mural that Logan saw the day before. A number of Anunnaki were standing in a circle near the centre of the room. Logan noticed that they weren't talking, just glancing at one another.

One member of the group broke away and nodded at John. They were led down a hallway to a room with the experimental plants and on to a much smaller room with the mushroom-shaped table.

It turned out that the mushroom table could change into a flat surface just by touching the top. When John laid out his plans, the ones retrieved from the farm, the table grew in size to accommodate all the pages. The walls and ceiling turned into a giant screen, onto which equations and schematic diagrams were displayed.

Ben was fascinated by the four Anunnaki who had followed them in. Along with the humans present, they were engrossed with the data streaming on the screens. Ben and Logan couldn't understand it, but the others appeared to comprehend and were pleased.

Scott turned away from the screen to his father, "Yes, okay, I understand some of it, the rest you can explain to me as we go along, but you haven't addressed the most important thing: what's the power source? For the life of me, I haven't been able to figure it out, and I'd say it's obvious you're going to need a whole power plant to get it to work. Any chance you have a power plant that I don't know about. Is there one down here we can use?"

John and Ed stared at Scott for a moment and started to laugh.

"You could say that," John was chuckling now. "This will be powered by the sphere, of course. I almost forgot you haven't seen it."

"Oh yeah, that's right," Ed said with a grin. "Prepare to be amazed!"

"Humph," Logan cleared his throat to get his grandfather's attention. "Once Dad sees the sphere, I think he'll have a lot of questions, so, is it okay if Ben and I take a look around this place? We're dying to see more of it."

John McCarthy looked over at one of the aliens, who inclined his head slightly, but didn't make a move. Another alien appeared at the door. He went up to the boys and indicated with a slight movement of the head that they should follow him.

Once again, the soft floors seemed to soak up any sound as Logan and Ben followed the alien along the passage. Three aliens passed by, nodding slightly as they went.

A nod for them is probably like us saying, 'Hello', Logan thought.

They continued to follow the passage as it spiralled downward. "You notice how we pass the elevator every once in a while, but there are no stairs," Ben said. "There doesn't seem to be a sharp turn anywhere, even their furniture is round. He lowered his voice, "I guess they don't like corners."

The Anunnaki leading the way stopped and stared at the two boys. An introduction of sorts followed. The name "Deefin" materialized in the teens' minds. It was as though they just knew his name. In return, Logan and Ben said their names aloud, gesturing at one another and speaking in painfully loud voices, as one might do when speaking to a non-English speaker.

Deefin waited a moment to allow two others to pass by. He placed his wrist against the wall. A narrow door slid open, and again they were struck by the size of the room.

Before them, as far as they could see, were animals of every kind in glass cages. As the boys walked around, they realized that these animals resembled many of the animals on earth, but in crazy ways. One looked like a large house cat, except that it had fangs, and its pale blue fur stood straight up in spikes. Another resembled a skunk, but it had more than one stripe and it was the size of a large dog. They spied the tiniest horse they had ever seen.

Intrigued, Ben walked over to the cage and put his hand on the glass. The animal crouched and backed away. It began to hiss and bare its tiny sharp teeth.

Surprised, Ben snatched his hand away. "Whoa! Hold on there, Shorty," he mumbled, "I'm leaving now."

Logan was a few rows over when he noticed what looked like a bear. It was larger than a grizzly bear and camouflaged with long green and brown hair.

"Is this one dangerous?" Logan called back to Deefin.

"Not to humans," answered Deefin. "But it would eat dogs, cats, squirrels, chipmunks, and many other smaller creatures that you have on Earth."

Logan waved his finger at the cage, "Not such a nice guy after all, are you?"

"He sounds like a Wayne or a Danny, always picking on the little guys," Ben said, recalling the neighbourhood bullies.

They wandered around for almost an hour before returning to the door. "Man, this place is awesome," exclaimed Ben to the Anunnaki, who was standing by, expressionless. "Are these the only animals you have?" he asked. "Do you have any more?"

"We do," Deefin affirmed. He waved his arm to direct them. "This way."

"It's funny, isn't it, the way you can hear them without them talking. Did you see him move his mouth?" whispered Logan to Ben.

"No, he didn't," Ben whispered back, "They definitely communicate using telepathy. Do you think your grandfather and Mr. Harris talk to them that way now?"

"Yeah, they must," Logan answered, "but if they can hear thoughts, can they read our minds?"

Deefin swivelled to face them, "Yes," he said, "but not always. Some thoughts can still be hidden. Still, we consider speech to be inefficient." The alien said all this without once moving his lips. "There is so much that you don't say aloud, though your minds chatter incessantly. And what you do say…"

Ben smiled. "I can hear you just like you were talking to me with your voice."

"So, is it alright if I ask what kind of thoughts can be hidden?" Logan asked, wondering if his thoughts had betrayed him.

The Anunnaki turned slightly to face Logan, "We are not used to strong emotions …or your spontaneous verbal outbursts… We find them …unsettling."

"Oh …geez, sorry about that," Ben apologized, "I guess that's just a human thing. We must seem kind of nuts to you sometimes."

"Yes, *kind of nuts*," confirmed Deefin. He stepped closer to Ben, until their faces were just a few inches apart. "Tell me," Deefin asked in his calm voice, "have you experienced a verbal outburst?"

Ben fidgeted as he replied, "Well, um, sure, just a couple of times when I was angry."

"Can I ask you another question?" Deefin continued.

"You said speech can be unreliable" Logan interjected. "What did you mean by that? How is it unreliable?"

"What a human verbalizes often does not agree with what he is thinking. Humans lie easily to one another," stated the Anunnaki. "This would be impossible for us."

"Yeah, it'd be impossible to lie," murmured Ben, who blushed a bright red.

"That is correct. This way, please," said Deefin, turning and continuing along the passage.

Ben elbowed Logan, "Do you think he might be listening to us right now?" he whispered, without taking his eyes away from Deefin.

"I can hear many thoughts at the same time," Deefin said as he came to a halt. Again, he pressed his wrist against the wall and stepped aside as the door whooshed open.

The teens could see that this room was a little different. It wasn't as bright as the others were. It was also smaller, but with a very high ceiling and walls that resembled a cave. Logan and Ben were expecting more animals, but this room was only for insects. They could see four glass cases with the ugliest creatures they'd ever seen and kept well back from an orange speckled bug that actually had teeth. It was continually jabbing, trying to bite the glass.

The boys decided to remain where they were, too nervous to venture any further.

"You are safe here," stated Deefin.

He must have read our minds, Logan thought. From now on, he would try not to give anything away. He and Ben glanced quickly at each other and nodded before moving closer to the next cage. They watched closely, as the smallest of the creatures tried unsuccessfully to climb up the side of the glass. It tried over and over again, and judging from the slime on the walls of its cage, the boys both concluded that it must have tried this at least a hundred times.

The final cage, at least three times the size of the others, was tucked into an alcove. The entire inside of the cage was webbed with silver threads, hiding the captive, and only allowing the outline of a dark shadow.

The boys crept closer. They were now only a few feet from the glass.

With terrifying speed, a huge black creature rushed out of the darkness and threw itself against the glass.

The boys wanted to scream. They opened their mouths, but not a sound escaped. The boys were mesmerized by the creature's baleful, human eyes. They were paralyzed.

The creature glared down at them. Thick, dark saliva drooled from its mouth and pooled onto the floor of the cage. It had rows of sharp teeth on the top and bottom of its mouth. Its body was bulbous and covered in dull, black hair, even the legs, which were clinging to the glass.

"Crootta!" said a voice behind the boys, cutting through the trance.

They grabbed each other for support.

Deefin seized the teens by the arms and shook them.

"This creature is called a 'Crootta'. Your John and Ed don't like it either. It can hypnotize you, make it impossible to move. I can guess what you saw." He continued, "Think of what terrorizes humans the most. It would be black, a reptile or insect. It would be a relentless, soul-less hunter, fierce, fearless, and lightning fast, with a rapacious appetite. Worse, it would feed on you slowly, delighting in your fear, your despondency, digesting you in pieces. This creature senses what we all fear and becomes that thing."

Ben rubbed his eyes. Deefin turned the boys away from the creature and began to force them to move away. Back at the door, the boys began to gasp.

Logan was breathing heavily as he tried to talk, "Are you sure that thing can't get out?"

"It cannot escape its enclosure," repeated Deefin. He tilted his head to the side as if receiving a message. "Come, they are ready to leave. We must go back now."

"Does that thing eat humans?" Ben asked, wide-eyed, and stumbling as he went.

Logan followed closely, constantly checking over his shoulder.

Deefin grabbed Ben and gently led him along the passage. "The Crootta will eat any creature. We have been searching for a suitable planet."

"As long as it's not this one," Logan said, walking faster.

"Yeah," agreed Ben, "and what happens if it does gets out?"

"It will not," answered Deefin. "One inch of Anunnaki glass is 10 inches of your human steel."

"Doesn't sound like enough for me," Ben whispered.

CHAPTER 31

"Yes, the Cioth are the most violent race we have ever come across," the Anunnaki explained. "Thousands of years ago, they were as humans are today on this planet. From time to time, they fought wars with their neighbours. The better their technology became, the more horrible the wars. Eventually, the three main powers formed an alliance to make peace. Of this we approved, but it didn't last. The powerful three began to dominate others, eventually stripping them of their natural resources. With their mastery of space travel, they have become very dangerous to the galaxy."

Suddenly, the room lit up. Writing appeared on the screens—one message in English, in Russian, in Hindi, Urdu, Japanese, Arabic, in every conceivable language. It trailed up the wall and across the ceiling. A sense of dread filled the room. The message read, "You will return what you have taken. You have ten earth days from this day and time. At the appointed hour, bring what is ours to the highest point on the island where you are holding it. Non-compliance will result in the poisoning of every human on this planet. Your citizens will remain in a deep sleep and others will join them. They will starve to death unless you return what is ours.

You will receive the antidote when we have the sphere aboard our ship. You have ten Earth days to comply."

The entire room fell silent, its occupants deep in thought for what seemed like a long time.

John got to his feet, "There isn't much time. We need to discover the antidote," he said, gazing around the table at the aliens. "And build my device," he nodded toward Ed and Scott. "We have to start now. I'm going to remain here and work on one part. It will be too heavy to move. Ed, if you could give me a hand here for a bit and then go over to the mainland to give Scott a hand to finish the other part, that'd be great."

Ed nodded. "And since we won't be taking any unnecessary chances at this point, you'll have to leave after dark."

Everyone got up and filed out of the room.

Back at the boat, John grasped Logan's shoulder and said, "We're going to need all the help we can get. I hope you boys will be ready if we need you."

"Do you want us to come back tonight to pick up Ed?" Logan asked.

John looked over at Scott, who nodded.

"Okay, we'll be back later, we can meet Ed here. You can count on us. We'll do anything to help," Logan assured him.

"Me, too," Ben added.

Later, a boat tore across the lake under an oppressive night sky. The cool air snapped at their clothes. Not a word was spoken.

CHAPTER 32

LOGAN'S MOTHER LEFT THE HOUSE a few hours after her husband and son that morning. She knew that the one-hour trip would have her arriving in Brockville around eight o'clock. Ted had told her to meet him at the warehouse.

She'd been there once with Scott, and with GPS to guide her she had no problem finding the place. It only took twenty minutes to pay for the part that Scott had ordered and have it loaded into the back of the SUV. Clad in nondescript cardboard and wrapped with two steel bands, it appeared to be nothing special.

Before she left Brockville, Cathy decided to stop and have lunch. This would be safe, she reasoned, because she was far enough away from Milford. She had eaten at this café before, she liked the food, and the waitress greeted everyone like an old friend. It buoyed her spirits and she was glad that she had stopped.

The drive back was eerie though, because each passing mile brought her closer to where the Cioth were poisoning her friends' children. Without realizing it, she began to slow down. Scott and Logan would not be home for hours, so she began searching for something, anything, to delay her return home. At last, she spied her favourite garden centre, where she pulled in. The place usually cheered her up. She hoped it would help to make her feel better, more hopeful, but after a brief stroll around the grounds, she realized that the place was practically empty. News of the sickness had spread. She purchased two plants and returned to her car, feeling no better.

A little while later, as she entered Milford, it occurred to her that she needed some groceries. With all that had been going on, she hadn't shopped in days. She chided herself: *why didn't I shop in Brockville?* It would have been safer.

Amidst a torrent of doubt, she failed to look in the review mirror: two armoured vehicles had just blocked the main road into town. The authorities were attempting to contain the sickness. The noose around Milford was tightening.

CHAPTER 33

IT WAS AT THE GROCERY store that she ran into Chief Constable Bailey. It made her feel safe to see him. Surely, no one would try anything with a police officer around. Besides, she would be careful. Surely, this would be enough.

"Hey, Cathy, how are you? I haven't seen you since you got back. How was the trip?" the Chief broke out in a big smile. He had a soft spot for Cathy ever since grade school.

"I'm good, and the trip was fascinating. How are you and Linda doing?" The two walked into the store together, chatting as they went.

"Orange Juice," someone just inside the door interrupted them. A young girl with a big smile and a tray stepped into their path. They recognized her, the daughter of the local pharmacist. Her smile was disarming as she greeted them by name. "Would you like to taste our freshly squeezed orange juice?" she beamed. "We squeeze it ourselves in the store everyday."

As they inquired after her dad, Cathy and the Chief each took the paper cup that she handed them.

They sipped the orange juice as they continued to talk.

Eventually, Cathy pointed at the dairy section, "I have to go this way," she said. "Don't forget to say hello to Linda for me."

"Sure will," said the Chief, "I hope I remember what she asked me to pick up!"

As Cathy left the store, she turned to see the Chief scratching his head, as if he'd forgotten something.

* * *

It only took Cathy a few minutes to get home from the store. She had bought two chrysanthemums from the garden center and returned to the car to get them. After taking them out of the car, she felt dizzy and her stomach began to churn. *It's probably from bending over*, she thought, *I'll get something to drink and lie down.* The dizziness made walking difficult, and Cathy stumbled along until everything began to get dark and fuzzy. The plants were getting heavier with each step, so she dropped them onto the grass beside the path. She was swaying now; it was getting harder to walk. Still, she made her way to the front door.

Suddenly an image came into her mind. Orange juice. *It's got to be. But that girl, I know her...* She fumbled for her cell phone and staggered inside. She accessed the directory and swept the display down to Scott's name. The cramps in her stomach were so bad that she doubled over. She was unaware that she had left the front door wide open, her mind seized on only one thing. Her phone lay on the threshold. She selected his name, dimly aware of the ringing. It went to voice mail. "Juice," was all she said.

The display timed out, Cathy's vision went black and she slipped into a coma.

CHAPTER 34

A LONG SHADOW CAST BY the boathouse greeted them. Scott realized that he and the boys had been gone the entire day. *Cathy would've been back ages ago,* he thought. He would have to tell her about everything he'd learned today.

As they tied the boat up, Scott reminded Ben about the need for secrecy.

Ben looked very serious as he nodded. "I know Mr. McCarthy, but nobody would believe me anyway!" With that, he jumped on his bike and rode off.

Scott's car was parked near the catwalk. The car ticked with the radiated heat from the afternoon sun.

"Ben's probably right," said Logan as he climbed into the passenger seat. "It does sound totally made up and crazy. And if I told anyone about the giant spider that scared me and Ben, no one would believe me in a million years."

Scott glanced sideways at his son. "Well, maybe that's a good thing. Can you imagine the mass panic if people knew what was happening in their own backyard?"

Logan didn't answer. He was staring out the window at the houses they were passing. He knew every family who lived along here, every single kid. "I wonder if anyone else got poisoned today," he murmured absently.

"I sure hope not." Scott frowned as he glanced quickly at Logan.

"So, I was wondering, Dad, what does Grampa's machine do? Is it something that will help?"

Scott continued to watch the road ahead, "Didn't your grandfather tell you when you were there yesterday?"

"No, he never even mentioned the machine, and I'm dying to know," Logan confessed. "Is it a secret?"

"Well, no, not from you, it isn't."

Scott slowed the car down as he began to say, "Okay, well, you know how the sphere can recognize a person by their DNA, right? That's how it knows that you and I are related to Grampa?"

"Sure," said Logan, "I've watched stuff about DNA on television. It can identify someone and how they're related. They can use it to catch criminals."

"Right, every living organism has DNA," explained Scott. "Your grandfather thinks that he's invented a machine that can detect alien DNA, the same way that the sphere can. Normally you would need a blood test or a hair or something to check DNA, but the machine can do it without even touching the person. Your grandfather started to worry about aliens and their intentions back when he found the sphere. It made him realize that aliens must have been coming here for hundreds of thousands of years. He thinks the majority of them mean us no harm, like the Anunnaki. But in case a species showed up that did mean us harm, your grandfather wanted us to have a means of identifying them. And, now, that time has come; they've arrived! These aliens, the Cioth, are virtually undetectable, because the Anunnaki say they look like humans, so Grampa's device will identify them, even when they're still out in space."

They had arrived home and were sitting in the driveway. Scott turned off the ignition, but made no move to exit the car, "And just so you know, Logan, the Anunnaki are doing all they can to find a cure for your friends. Still, you'll have to be on your guard until that happens. And one other thing, let's try to stay positive for your mother, okay?"

They were parked directly behind Cathy's car. Scott spotted something in the back of the SUV. "Looks like your mom picked up that part for me." Together they unloaded and carried it to the garage door.

"I'll go in and open the garage door," Logan said as he left to open the front door.

"Hey, Dad, it's open. Maybe Mom just got home?"

"Ughh, great," his father groaned. "Can you hurry up now? This thing is getting heavy."

"Scott! Scott!" It was Brian Littman from across the street, running toward them with Darth on a leash. "Look, I'm sorry to have to tell you." Brian took a big breath. "Cathy was taken to the hospital, a few hours ago. I saw that your front door was wide open when I got home from work, and a while later I noticed that it was still open, so I came over to investigate. Cathy was on the floor in the hallway, unconscious, so I called an ambulance. She's at Milford General."

* * *

Scott banged his fist on the steering wheel. The drive to the hospital seemed to take an eternity. "She should have come with us," Scott said. "I can't believe I left her here alone while these aliens are poisoning people all over town."

His cell phone buzzed, message waiting. His mind was elsewhere. He accelerated hard.

CHAPTER 35

IT WAS TWILIGHT WHEN THEY arrived. A breeze had come up and was rustling the tops of the giant Norway maple trees that ringed the hospital.

Scott's car skidded to a halt in the parking lot. Logan and his father vaulted a small fence and ran for the front doors. The two barged into the reception area and came to an abrupt halt. It was a shock to see so many people they knew in the waiting area.

From the nurses' station, Chief Bailey's wife, Linda, came rushing up to them. "Oh, Scott!" she cried. "I've been trying to get a hold of you. The doctors think that they were either drugged or poisoned—they're not sure. It wasn't an accident, of that, they're certain. Who would want to poison the chief? He's very popular, and everyone loves Cathy. Did you hear that they were in the same place this afternoon? The grocery store." She was talking so fast that Scott and Logan could hardly keep up.

A woman came up to them. "Do you see this? Can you believe it? Someone is trying to poison the whole town!" Her head dropped and she began to cry. "Everyone here had a family member in the store this afternoon, so that's where it must have happened." She shook her head. "No one knows what to do, and now the military has quarantined the town. I honestly don't know how that will help, but it's obvious that something really horrible is going on around here."

At the reception desk Scott gave their names. It wasn't long before a nurse appeared and asked Scott and Logan to follow her. She led them to a small room, where they were made to scrub their hands and don gowns, gloves and facemasks.

"They're in the ICU. Come this way," she instructed. She ushered them through two sets of doors to the intensive care unit.

The ICU was large, with rooms on either side. There were several beds jammed into each room, a concession to the reality of the spreading sickness. Every bed was separated by a curtain and there were monitors flashing blue numbers, each beeping innumerable alarm conditions. The patients were attached to intravenous tubes and bags of clear fluid. It was an effort to do something, the standard response, anything to allay fears and suggest hope.

At one door, the nurse paused and glanced inside. Logan nodded, tight-lipped and went in. He approached his mother's bed and his anxiety grew. Cathy was lying very still with her arms by her sides.

Leaning over her, the nurse shone a tiny flashlight into his mother's eyes. "We're keeping her hydrated," said the nurse.

There was a larger tube in her mouth; it was taped to her cheek. The nurse told them that she was in a coma.

She still smelled of her favourite soap and to Logan it looked like she could have been sleeping.

As the nurse turned to leave, she gave the two a weak smile. She had seen too many of these cases.

Logan stepped closer and was about to touch his mother's hand when he stopped. *How was this possible?* After all, he had seen her that morning. She was fine. Now her skin was very pale. It looked like candle wax, except around her eyes, where it was a brilliant red. There were her veins, bright blue and visible everywhere, protruding from her face and her arms and hands.

Logan carefully picked up his mother's hand and held it. "Mom," he whispered, "wake up. Okay? Can you hear me? Try to wake up." It was awkward. He hadn't held her hand since he was a young boy.

Scott was on the other side of the bed. He gently stroked Cathy's arm and squeezed his eyes shut for a moment.

"I'm really sorry, son, I don't think we're going to get her to wake up right now. And I had no idea that she was going to look like this. You really shouldn't have to see this. I think…"

"No," Logan blurted, "I'm not leaving." He gave his father a defiant look.

"I wish you would do me this favour, please," his father said. "Go and wait for me in the waiting room. I don't think your mother would want you to see her like this. You know I'm right."

Seeing the look of anguish on his father's face, Logan decided not to argue. He squeezed his mother's hand and whispered, "Mom, everything's going to be okay. Dad, Grampa and a lot of other….er, people are working on it. I know they're going to find a cure. Don't worry. I'm going to be back tomorrow." He kissed her on the forehead in parting.

Slowly and quietly, he walked away, glancing at each bed as he passed. Only close relatives were allowed in the ICU. He'd been told this when he wanted to see Darcy. But now that he was here, this could be the perfect opportunity to check on Katy and Darcy.

There were many patients, and it didn't seem as though he would be able to find them, until he remembered that they were the first victims of the poison. If the patients were being lined up as they came in, perhaps Darcy and Katy would be at the far end of the room. He finally located Darcy. He was surrounded by family. They were talking very quietly to him, perhaps in the hope that he could hear their voices. They looked so sad that Logan decided not to intrude. He averted his eyes, only to see Katy in the next bed.

It was shocking to see that Katy was in the same condition as his mother. She had the pale skin and the red around the eyes, and the bright blue veins. Katy's father was collapsed in a chair, leaning forward with his head on the bed. At first, Logan thought that he might have fallen asleep, but when he got closer, he realized that the professor was praying.

Much as he wanted to spend a little time with his friends, if only to whisper something encouraging in their ear, he knew that this wasn't the right time, and left.

As quiet as church. That was the waiting room filled with relatives, each of them praying for some positive news. Logan was like them—with one difference—he knew what the doctors were up against, a terrible Cioth poison. He was also aware of how bad things could become, unless the Anunnaki could find an antidote for a poison they'd never seen before. The only other way to save everyone, Logan knew, would be to hand over a powerful weapon and his grandfather to a vicious alien race.

CHAPTER 36

THE RIDE HOME WAS QUIET. Both father and son were deep in their own roiling thoughts and fears.

Logan's father looked dead tired. From the outset, it had been a roller coaster ride for him: first, happiness at being reunited with his father after a year of believing he was dead, then the excitement at meeting the Anunnaki in their underground facility, then sheer dread inspired by the awful Cioth threat. Finally, there was the gut-wrenching personal consequence of not yielding to the threat: returning home to find that Cathy was one of the Cioth's victims.

As soon as they walked through the front door, Scott grew energized, proceeded directly to the basement and started to drag up everything he would need to build Grampa's device.

"Ceilings aren't high enough down there," he said, his voice cracked with emotion. "Can you give me a hand? We can set up our equipment in the garage."

Logan helped carry everything up from the basement and watched his father transform the garage into a lab.

It was night. Logan slipped out of the house and rode to the marina. He had almost forgotten about Ed.

He'd promised his grandfather that he would pick Ed up, and here he was leaving the house at the exact time that he should be arriving on the island.

At the marina, Logan took the turn too fast and skidded into the parking lot. He lost control on the gravel and collided with another bike. The other rider had seen him coming and jumped off.

He lay there on the ground for a moment, trying to decide if he was still in one piece. He raised himself onto one elbow. Someone ran toward him from the bushes and dropped onto his knees beside Logan.

"Are you all right, son?" It was Ed Harris!

The owner of the other bike was peeking over Ed's shoulder. "Not my fault, you were going too fast, that's why you were unable to stop," stated the other rider matter-of-factly.

"You think?" Logan remarked, preparing to get up. He was still surveying the damage when he recognized the other rider.

"Are you sure you're okay?" Ed asked, as he helped Logan to his feet. "Maybe we should get you somewhere where you can sit down."

"No, I'm okay, but how did you get here? I was just going over to the island to pick you up. Did Ben get you? He should have called me."

"No, I haven't seen Ben," Ed replied. He looked around. "Look, Logan, if you're okay, I'd like to get going." He walked over to the bushes and hoisted a large duffle bag over his shoulder.

Logan stood with some difficulty, "So, Ben didn't call you, either?"

"No, he didn't, but no worries, I managed to hitch a ride." He held out his hand to Logan, "Can you walk? We really have to go."

"Take my bike." It was the oddly dressed girl. She had righted both bikes and now stood between them. She pushed her bike forward to emphasize the invitation.

"What are you doing here?" Ed asked, peering at the girl.

Logan noticed the queer expression on Ed's face.

"I will leave now," she answered as she let Ed take the bike from her. Ed nodded as if in agreement, although less composed than usual.

By then, the girl had disappeared into the dark.

"Huh. Well, okay, we've got wheels," Ed said to Logan. "Now let's get out of here, before someone spots me and thinks they've seen a ghost."

"What was that all about? You know her?"

"Know her? I'm just glad she had a bike. Let's go!"

On the way home, Logan realized that the cut on his arm was deeper than he thought. It was hurting like crazy, and when he looked down, there was quite a lot of blood around the rip in his shirt.

"Yeah, we'll have to see to that when we get to your house," Ed told him, after following his gaze. "Do you know if there have been any other cases of poisoning today?"

"Yes, Mom's in the hospital," Logan told a shocked Ed Harris. "She's in a coma like everyone else, including some of my friends. Chief Constable Bailey, too."

"I'm really sorry Logan, you know we'll do everything we can," Ed tried to reassure him. "The

Anunnaki are thousands of years ahead of us. I'm sure they'll be able to help."

I hope you're right, Logan thought to himself. The trouble was that the Cioth were poisoning humans. How much did the Anunnaki know about curing humans? And did he just hear a touch of uncertainty in Ed's voice?

* * *

Scott was dragging heavy equipment across the garage floor. He was almost finished setting things up. Darth was lying on a blanket nearby, one eye was open and following every move that Scott made.

As soon as Ed stepped through the door, Darth began to whimper with delight. He jumped up and dashed over to Ed, who bent down to hug the dog and was knocked flat on his back. Moments later, the dog discovered the bag that Ed had carried over his shoulder from the marina and began to push it around, trying to get it open, all the while sniffing madly.

"Food," Ed explained. He picked the bag up and held it out of the dog's reach. "We thought it best that you not buy anything. The Anunnaki sent this. I think you'll be surprised how good it is, even if it does look a little strange. And don't worry my friend, there's something in here for you, too," he reassured the dog. Ed reached inside the bag and pulled out an item wrapped in blue cloth. After opening it, he tossed a small piece to Darth and handed the rest to Logan. "Try one of these, they're really good for you, in fact it will help speed up the healing time." He was pointing at the blood on Logan's shirt.

Taking the small package of food, Logan could see that it was wrapped in a green organic substance that resembled crushed grass. The food was blue and shaped like a pancake, with grooves like tree bark. It couldn't have looked more unappetizing.

The men talked as Scott cleaned and bandaged Logan's arm, insisting that he go to bed soon and let them work.

"Yeah, okay," Logan agreed reluctantly, "this stupid cut is really starting to sting." Before leaving the room, Logan stopped and turned around. "Look, I know the Cioth are bad and everything, but isn't there some way to give them the sphere, but save Grampa?"

Ed wore a solemn expression. He studied Logan's face for a moment. "I know how tempting that might seem Logan, but the Cioth aren't just bad, they are incredibly cruel. There's no guarantee that they'll hand over the antidote once they have the sphere. The Anunnaki told us that the Cioth conquer other planets, and each time they do they enslave all of the inhabitants. After they have taken everything, all the resources, they lay waste to the planet. Within weeks, the planet's inhabitants starve. We probably would have been next, were it not for the Anunnaki." He paused and swallowed hard. "We're afraid that if the Cioth obtain the sphere, their ability to ruin a planet will be multiplied a thousand times. No one in the galaxy would be safe."

Logan slumped against the door and folded his arms. "All I want is for Mom, Darcy and Katy and everybody else to get better. I feel like all we're doing is sitting around and waiting until the Anunnaki figure out how to cure everybody, if they can."

"I'm just as concerned about your mother and everyone else as you, son," his father reassured him. "You know we're all going to work as hard and as fast as we can."

"Yeah, I know, I know," Logan turned to walk away, shaking his head and cradling his injured arm. The repeated reassurances were getting somewhat less reassuring.

In his room, Logan drank a little warm milk and took a small bite of the alien pancake. It was sweet, crunchy and had a slightly lemony taste. Before he knew it, it was all gone, and his stomach felt full. As soon as his head hit the pillow, he fell into a deep sleep.

CHAPTER 37

THE NEXT MORNING, LOGAN ROSE to a silent house. He was used to hearing the radio and sounds of cooking coming from the kitchen. He rounded the corner and saw the two men, rumpled and tired from working all night, now seated at the breakfast table.

Sunlight was pouring in through the kitchen window. On the counters, Logan noticed all the Anunnaki food now sealed in plastic containers.

"Morning Logan," the two men said at once. They'd been eating the Anunnaki pancakes.

Logan raised his arm and waved.

Scott leaned back in his chair and stretched his arms high above his head. He rubbed his face and checked his phone for messages. When he listened to Cathy's message, he sighed. His wife's last words before she sank into a coma: "Juice." He bit his lip and put the phone down. *This confirmed what he had been thinking: it's an orally administered poison.* He glanced at Ed and Logan and conveyed the grim news.

He steeled himself. "There's still work to do on your grandfather's machine. It's complicated. I'm really concerned about being able to finish on time."

"We have to, that's all there is to it," Ed's voice was firm. "We have no choice but to keep going." He grabbed some food off the plate and stood up. "But first, I think I'm going to try to grab a nap; then I'll carry on here…while you visit Cathy."

Scott nodded, "Sounds good. You can take the guest room next to the bathroom, and if there's anything you need, just holler." He paused for a second, "We are all going to have to watch what we drink—anything liquid, Logan. That's how they poisoned your mother."

The room fell silent.

"I wish…" Logan started to say when he was startled by a loud knock at the front door.

Ed's eyes opened wide. "Wait! Remember, whoever that is, they mustn't see me."

Scott whispered to Logan, "You answer it, okay, but see who it is first."

The door from the garage led to the kitchen and beyond to the hall, where Logan had a good view of the front door. At the top of the door was a small window where Logan could usually see the top of a visitor's head. Seeing nothing, he leaned over and peeked cautiously through the side window.

It was Ben. His back was to the door and he was shuffling nervously from one foot to the other. Logan flung the door open.

CHAPTER 38

"My parents are in the hospital!" Ben sniffed.

"What?" Logan pulled Ben into the house.

"Yes, they got sick last night, really sick. I had to call an ambulance. Now both of them are in a coma. I've been at the hospital all night. I was going to go home, but I don't want to—there's nobody there. Is it okay if I stay with you?"

"Absolutely," said Scott, who had just stepped into the hallway. "Of course you can stay with us, for as long as you need to."

"Yeah, you can share my room," Logan added, "My mom is in the hospital too, she got sick yesterday, along with Chief Bailey, and a bunch of other people at the grocery store."

"Oh, man, I'm really sorry," Ben said as he followed Logan into the kitchen, where he flopped into a chair.

"Try not to worry, Ben," Scott patted Ben's shoulder, "I'm going to take a nap, but Logan will look after you."

"Thanks," Ben mumbled as he crossed his arms and slumped further down in the chair. "It was horrible," Ben told Logan. "I thought my parents were going to die. I sat at the hospital all night, and I didn't know what to do. The doctor told me stuff, but I don't remember.

I started to watch everyone, you know, the doctors and nurses, and the people in the waiting room. They were drinking coffee, and eating stuff, and I couldn't tell them not to. And now I'm starving, but I'm afraid to eat."

"Don't worry, you can eat here. We've got lots of food, Anunnaki food," Logan told him. "Mr. Harris is here, and he brought over some food from the island. I ate some last night—it's pretty good. I'll get you some."

"Okay," Ben looked distracted, "I wish I could have told them what was going on, but I didn't. Oh! You'll never believe who was at the hospital when I got there at two o'clock in the morning. It was that weird girl. She was sitting in the waiting room, and I'm sure she was watching me. Do you think she could be one of them, one of the Cioth?"

Logan had been putting some of the alien food on a plate, one of the 'pancakes' and two small red things that looked like the mushroom caps.

"I doubt it. I don't think the Cioth would ever do anything to help us out. She was at the marina, last night I guess, before she went to the hospital. She gave her bike to Ed, so he didn't have to walk here. Besides that, I doubt the Cioth would want any attention, right? Look at the way she dresses, everybody notices her everywhere she goes."

"Yeah, I guess," said Ben. He was looking suspiciously at the food that Logan had just placed in front of him. "What is this stuff?"

Watching Ben's reaction, Logan rolled his eyes, "Give it a try. Honest, it's not bad."

Ben took a tiny bite of the 'pancake' and jumped to his feet. "Yuk, that's rotten," he cried.

Logan was shocked. In the next moment though, Ben grinned and dropped back into his seat.

"Just kidding," he chuckled, waving the 'pancake' in the air. "This is kind of good."

Logan punched Ben on the shoulder. "You're an idiot, Kaplan!"

"Uh-huh," Ben agreed, but his smile quickly faded, "Listen, did Mr. Harris say anything about how the Anunnaki are doing, finding a cure for the poison? I'm freaking out about my parents and everybody. Did you see what they look like? Zombies, all of them. I remember one of the doctors at the hospital told me that apart from throwing up, they can't find anything wrong with them, except, that they look awful and they just won't wake up. They don't know why it's happening."

"Yeah, believe me, I know. I'd sure like to get my hands on one of those Cioth. Beat the crap out of him."

"Yeah, sure, no problem. Didn't you hear what Ed said? They're warriors. They go around conquering entire planets. Do you really think we can do anything against them?"

"Well, maybe not. But I still want to see if I can maybe spot one, so we know what they look like."

"That's a great idea," Ben smirked, "but do you really think we'll know one when we see one?"

"We might if we hang around where there's sure to be one. You know, like a restaurant or a grocery store, that's where they've been poisoning people, sooner or later one is sure to show up, don't you think?"

Ben gave Logan a strange look, "You haven't been paying attention, have you? Nobody is eating in a restaurant anymore. They're afraid, so the restaurants are closing, the grocery stores, too. They're trucking food into Milford now. Look at us, we're eating alien food!"

"Geez!" Logan glared at his friend, "Why don't you suggest something for once? Everybody is sick, so what do you want to do, stay home and watch TV?"

"No, I don't," Ben shook his head, "and maybe it's a good idea to be able to spot one. That way we can stay away from them. I just don't know where to look," Ben continued, "and what if they spot us first, and figure out what we're doing?"

Logan was starting to look around as he answered, "I'm pretty sure they won't kill us, because of the Anunnaki. It helps when you've got one of these!" He pulled out his phone. "We're going to take some pictures!"

CHAPTER 39

AFTER TAKING A SHORT NAP, the boys left the house. Mr. Einhorn spotted them immediately. He was walking around his front yard with his usual cup of coffee in hand.

"Logan, Logan," he yelled, trying to wave them over. "Sorry about your mother. How's your father doing?"

"He's fine," Logan yelled back, before turning and walking quickly away. He had no intention of listening to his neighbour trying to blame his mom and dad for the poisoning.

"Humph," Einhorn grunted his irritation. He narrowed his eyes at the boys as they walked away. He found it hard to believe that Logan wasn't sick yet. The boy looked fine to him, but wasn't it Scott and Cathy McCarthy who brought the sickness to Milford? It had to be. After all, didn't it show up right after they got back from their trip?

"And you'll notice, Ivy," Einhorn told his wife that morning, "that nobody outside of Milford has gotten sick. Am I right?" Einhorn eyed his wife, who always agreed with him.

"I say they should quarantine the McCarthys in a hospital somewhere, so they can't infect anyone else. I saw in the paper this morning," he continued, "that they still don't know what this thing is or where it came from. Isn't that ridiculous? Here Scott goes around digging up weird stuff all over the planet, this time it was alien bones, and the health department says they don't know where this came from, unbelievable! It's as plain as the nose on your face, and I actually told them to look at the McCarthys, but they didn't believe me."

"And, do you know what else they said? 'Don't worry, because there will be food brought in from out of town.' They are going to empty out the grocery store, probably destroy all the old food. People will have to go over to the recreation centre to get a bag of the new stuff that they're bringing in. I'll bet you anything it will be expensive, and you know what else, they want us to empty out our kitchens and replace every bit of food. Who has the money for that? All I can say is, somebody must be making a lot of money from this. I'd sure like to know who."

"Well, dear," ventured Ivy with some caution, "we do want to be careful, don't we? I know I don't want to get sick."

"Sure," Einhorn was waving his arms around, "but how do we know that we have anything that's poison? We might be throwing out perfectly good food, spending lots of money when we don't have to."

"As far as I'm concerned, this is their fault," Ivy grumbled, as she jabbed her finger toward the McCarthy house. "They are the ones who should be paying."

"Damn right," Einhorn agreed, as they both glared at the house next door. "The McCarthys and their kid are nothing but trouble. Even old John McCarthy, when he was alive, always showing off how smart he was."

* * *

It was mid-afternoon when boys returned, having had no luck in locating and photographing any of the Cioth. Their neighbour, Mr. Einhorn, was watching from his porch. The boys hurried into the house. No one had paid much attention to the dog over the past few days, so Logan let him loose in the backyard to chase squirrels.

Meanwhile, Einhorn had retrieved a bowl from the kitchen that contained four small mounds of food. After checking that the coast was clear, he took it outside, between the two houses, where it was very easy to stay out of sight. Einhorn held up the plate of food and quietly waved Darth over. "Here boy, come and get it."

Darth watched the neighbour for a minute. He could smell the food, but he was suspicious. This was the man who always yelled and chased him with a newspaper.

"Aww, there's a good boy. See, I have a nice little treat for you," he said as sweetly as possible. He waved the dish around. Still Darth watched from a distance.

"Come on you stupid dog, I want you to test something for me," he called in a singsong voice. "You are really going to like this."

The dog looked on.

Finally, Einhorn reached over the fence and put the plate on the ground. Darth's head came up and he stared at the plate. A moment later, when Einhorn backed well away, the dog crept forward a little. "Okay, I get it, you little mongrel. You don't trust me… I'll just stay here and let you eat in peace. Be sure to let me know if it's been poisoned, won't you?"

Back in the house, Einhorn spoke to his wife, "These cartons on the counter are the ones I'm testing on the dog. See, I put red check marks on them. By tomorrow, we'll know if there was any poison. I think this is a good way of testing all of our food, don't you?"

"I guess so," Ivy agreed: no surprise there.

"Has to be," Einhorn nodded. "It's the only thing that makes sense. So, if McCarthy is going to endanger all of us, we can at least use his dog as a guinea pig."

At the side of the house, Darth approached the food and sniffed.

CHAPTER 40

It took twenty minutes to get to the hospital, just in time for visiting hours. They chained their bikes to the rack near the front entrance and proceeded to the intensive care unit on the second floor. Logan showed Ben where to find the gowns, masks and slippers needed for the ICU.

After checking in with the nurse, they each went their separate ways, Ben to see his mother and father, who were in side-by-side beds, and Logan to visit his mother. Because of the growing numbers of people affected, the ICU had swelled to consume the entire floor.

Logan sat and talked to his mother for a while until a nurse came to check on her. "Can she hear me when I talk to her?" he asked. It was a common question these days.

Still, the nurse smiled kindly at him, "We're not really sure, but just in case, I would continue to talk to her, if I were you."

As the nurse continued to watch Logan, she decided that a few words of hope might be a good thing. Over the last few days, she had seen young kids and teenagers trying to cope with having a sick mother or father, or in some cases, both parents. "I want you to know," she said quietly to Logan, "that there are some incredibly clever doctors working on this right now, so try not to worry so much."

She cast her gaze around the room, and back down at Cathy, "It's like they've eaten the witch's apple, they've fallen asleep and they can't wake up." Without thinking, these words spilled out of her mouth.

She turned to leave, and, immediately regretting what she'd just said, turned back to say, "Your mother is doing fine now, she just doesn't seem ready to wake up." She couldn't bring herself to tell him about the patient who died overnight.

* * *

After an hour and a half of talking to his comatose mother about how she need not worry about them because they had safe food, that he would do the dishes, take out the trash, and do better at school, he would learn much later that this was part of the grieving process—bargaining. It would also only occur to him much later this was the most time he'd ever spent talking to his mother.

An anxious voice in another room was raised enough for Logan to hear. "Darcy, Darcy, can you hear me? It's Mom." He would never have recognized Mrs. Ryder in the hospital mask and gown. She was clutching Darcy's hand and talking to him in a loud voice. "Please, son wake up!"

One of the nurses hurried over and tried to console her, "Mrs. Ryder, I know how worried you are, believe me, and I want you to know that we are doing everything we can." Her voice tightened in telling this lie. In fact, everything wasn't enough.

Mrs. Ryder looked dazed. She looked at the nurse as though she didn't realize that the woman was talking to her. Over the nurse's shoulder, she spotted Logan. She rushed over and grabbed his hand, "Oh Logan, I'm so glad you're here. Come and talk to Darcy. It'll be good for him to hear your voice."

As Darcy's mother pulled Logan closer to the bed, the nurse whispered to him, "Please, can you stay with them for a while? Every bit helps."

Darcy looked like Logan's mother and Katy, with red eyes and protruding veins. It was hard to see his friend so sick and helpless. Logan did as he was asked and whispered in his friend's ear. "Listen buddy, I hope you can hear me, because, believe it or not, my grandfather and Ed are back. Right now, there are a whole lot of, um, aliens, yup you were right, actual aliens, who are working to make you better. All you have to do is hang in there, okay?"

When Logan heard mumbling behind him, he turned around to find Ben standing with Darcy's mother. He was trying to reassure her, too, "I know that Darcy's going to be okay. He's a really strong guy, and I'll bet you anything that the doctors will find a cure soon."

Mrs. Ryder was staring down at Darcy and only half listening, "Look at him. I'm so scared." She began to cry just as her husband came up behind her.

Mr. Ryder turned her around and hugged her, stroking her back. Over her shoulder, he gave a weak smile and spoke to Logan and Ben. "Thanks for coming guys, it means a lot to us to see Darcy's friends."

"He's like our brother," Logan affirmed, with Ben nodding in agreement.

Later, after leaving Darcy, they decided to go in search of Katy. The nurses didn't seem interested in stopping them. They were overwhelmed by the number of patients.

They found Katy, further down the hall in a room with a number of women and girls of different ages. It struck Logan right away how small she looked lying there, like a five-year-old with blue magic marker on her face. After seeing his mom and Darcy, and now Katy, he grew angry. Without realizing it, he clenched his fists. All he wanted was to go out and find a Cioth, and do whatever it took to make him give them the antidote.

"Come on," Ben yanked on Logan's arm. "I think we should go now. We can come back tomorrow, okay? Let's just get out of here."

They threw their masks and gowns into a bin and proceeded down the long hall toward the exit. Ever since they had left the change room though, Ben felt the buzz starting in his head. Something was wrong.

CHAPTER 41

IF SHE'D BEEN DRESSED NORMALLY, like any other girl her age, he might not have noticed her, but she was still wearing the oversized clothes and the rumpled ball cap. They were almost past when Ben spotted her, the girl who had crashed into him at the Porthole and later shoved him into the water at the marina. She was slumped in a chair, biting her nails while glaring at something across the room. Her gaze was so intense that she didn't notice them.

Ben tapped Logan on the arm and stopped. He indicated the girl with a jerk of his head. "Look who's here," he said, not taking his eyes off her.

"Oh, yeah," Logan chuckled, "it's the girl with the bike. There must be someone here she knows, probably someone in her family."

Logan started to walk away, but Ben stopped him. "I want to talk to her."

It was as though the girl felt Ben's gaze, because she looked up. She didn't seem nervous or surprised when she spotted him, but suddenly her eyes began to dart back and forth between Ben and the opposite corner of the room. He stayed where he was as he tried to figure out what she was doing. What did she want; did she expect him to trust her? She was sitting a little forward now, tapping her nails furiously. She jerked her head toward the opposite corner.

Something about her look convinced Ben to follow her gaze. To where? There were only two men sitting together in the corner. They were both tall, slim and yet athletic looking. He glanced back at the girl and shrugged – maybe it was a stupid game.

Finally, the girl got up and walked purposefully toward him. She passed by very slowly. "It's *them*," she whispered, "I've been watching them. Can't you see?"

Logan overheard the remark, and now both boys were staring intently at the two men. As they stared, they began to wonder, did this girl know who the Cioth were? Was she actually trying to say that these men were Cioth? When they looked back at the men, something did indeed seem strange. Both men were wearing sunglasses, and why wear them in a room where the curtains were closed. Their posture was perfect, in a room full of slouching, round-shouldered, despondent relatives. They wore no expressions as they gazed at everyone around them.

The boys turned to each other, "Is it possible? Are you thinking what I'm thinking?" Logan asked.

"Yeah, I might be, but how would we know for sure? And how come that girl knows?"

"Maybe she's psychic. Anyway, in case she's right, we could wait for them to leave and follow them, see where they go?" Logan hadn't taken his eyes off the men.

"They might be here all night," protested Ben. "I don't think your dad would like that."

"Maybe I can do something to make them leave," Logan gave Ben a sly grin.

"How are you going to do that? Light their chairs on fire?"

"No, I'll just do this," Logan pulled out his phone and took a picture of the two men. The flash drew people's attention; they turned to see what was going on. The two men stared at Logan but didn't move.

"I don't think that it's working." Ben dropped his gaze to the floor, "We might be wrong about them."

"We'll see," said Logan, who spun around and started to leave. Ben followed. They left the room and walked quickly down the main corridor, only to fall back into one of the rooms.

The two strangers got up and headed for the door.

Logan and Ben paused until the men were well ahead in the corridor and followed them.

CHAPTER 42

BEN SENSED THAT THE GIRL was right. The buzzing in his head had gotten much louder as the men passed them in the corridor. Odd, he had just realized that there was no buzzing when the girl had stood next to him.

In front of the hospital, there were many people sitting on benches, others standing around talking and smoking. It was the overflow from the waiting room. The day had at last surrendered to the night and the number of people had mushroomed as the sickness tightened its grip on the town. Harsh fluorescent lighting added a blue note to the scene, adding to the encroaching chill.

The strangers were standing off to one side, concealed behind one of the large white pillars that held up a portico. For a moment, the boys couldn't see them, but after taking a few steps along the walkway, the strangers came into view and their eyes locked on the teens.

The men were moving again. Logan gave Ben's arm a pull—he was determined to see where they were going.

At the far side of the hospital, the men turned into a long driveway sandwiched between the hospital's main building and the parking garage.

Logan and Ben were getting close, but at the end of the driveway, they stopped. The lights in the parking garage provided scant illumination. If it weren't for four rectangles of light from the second-floor windows of the hospital, it would be completely dark. They boys crept cautiously forward, staying as close as possible to the wall, away from the light. They were midway along when someone in a room above switched a light off. From this point on, it was very hard to see. Now they felt vulnerable. They could either run to the far end of the driveway, and risk catching up to the two men, or turn back.

"Can we go back? I don't think I want to go any farther," Ben whispered.

"Yeah, good idea, but at least we know what they look like now. We have a picture. Let's go." Logan turned to follow Ben, who was already edging his way back along the wall.

Suddenly, directly in their path, someone stepped onto the driveway. He was standing very erect with his arms straight down by his sides, and even though Logan and Ben were hidden in darkness, he appeared to be looking them in the eye. The boys held their breath and stood frozen in place. The man was in silhouette, but his stature and a tiny glint off his glasses told them what they didn't want to know. He began to march toward them.

Logan spun Ben around and prepared to run in the other direction, when a second man appeared in one of the rectangles of light. They were trapped.

With nowhere to go, Logan and Ben pressed themselves against the wall. Ben tried to yell, but nothing came out, his voice was gone, his throat constricted so tight it hurt to swallow. The men were now only a few feet away. Both boys turned their heads to the side and squeezed their eyes shut.

CHAPTER 43

OFF IN THE DISTANCE LOGAN could hear a wailing sound, but before his vision cleared and his brain could figure out what it meant, he was picked up and smashed against the wall. His eyes popped open, and there before him was something unexpected.

The alien was about six feet tall with perfect facial features. Up close, he reminded Logan of a comic book character, a hero with a straight nose, strong jaw, and thick blond hair.

Somewhere out of his field of vision, Ben was moaning. Ben, too, had been pinned against the wall and dropped, where he was now, his face in the weeds beside the driveway.

Now, Logan felt himself being hoisted into the air. The Cioth was holding him up at arms length by one hand, and staring him in the eyes. "Ten days," said a diffused voice. "Tell him."

The Cioth glared at Logan for a second and spewed a luminous gas into his face. In what seemed a contemptuous gesture, he lifted him higher before dropping him to the ground.

Another noise pressed into Logan's awareness. Fear had made it impossible to think, but now Logan recognized a sound, an ambulance siren? The aliens' expressions had remained neutral this whole time, but now they exchanged cautious looks.

Logan rolled to one side. He saw Ben sprawled on the pavement, but was only dimly aware of the bright, flashing lights stabbing into the alley at the far end. The wailing grew to a crescendo. A large vehicle careened toward them.

Frantic horn blaring and the screech of brakes finally tore the aliens' attention away from the boys. With only yards to spare, the Cioth stepped out of the path of the ambulance, and faded into the night.

The ambulance skidded to a stop beside Logan and Ben. A window rolled down and an angry voice called out, "Take your fight somewhere else. Can't you read? This driveway is for ambulances!"

Ben crawled over beside Logan. "I - I can't get up," an unmistakable pitch of terror tinged his voice.

Neither could move for several minutes. Ben was struggling to get his legs underneath him. Logan groaned and rolled onto his stomach, anxious to get to his feet.

"We have to get out of here, Ben. They might decide to come back!" His vision was blurred and beginning to dim.

* * *

Time passed. They stumbled along, not stopping until they spilled through the hospital's main doors into the entrance hall.

A nurse called out to them, "Can we help you?"

Logan stopped and turned to face her.

She gasped. "Oh dear! What happened to your face, is that a burn?" The nurse rushed around the desk to get a closer look, "What is this stuff?" she asked, as she touched the slime with the tip of her finger. "Never mind, we need to wash it off, come with me." Then she realized her mistake, "This stuff burns!"

After gently washing his face several times with something the nurse had given him, Logan's face still felt hot. The doctor on duty thought it was a chemical burn and wanted to know how it happened. Logan stared at the man. He didn't know what to say. Ben sputtered, "Something tipped over in the garage and splattered him."

Before they knew it, the doctor was calling Logan's father, who happened to be right there in the hospital visiting his wife. "I've given him something for the burn. Make sure he applies it three times a day," the doctor advised. "His skin is going to peel—this resembles a bad sunburn—but I have to say, whatever chemical this was, you should really think about locking it up or disposing of it altogether. It's dangerous."

Scott was confused. As soon as the doctor left the room, he turned to his son, "What chemical was he talking about?" he demanded to know. "I don't have anything that would do this. What on Earth happened to you?" It was an oddly apt remark.

Logan took a deep breath, he was holding onto the side of the bed, "Is it okay if I tell you at home? I just need to go home, now."

"Me, too," Ben agreed, in a defeated whisper.

CHAPTER 44

SITTING AT THE KITCHEN TABLE, with a glass of pale green milk-like drink in front of them, Logan and Ben recounted the entire experience at the hospital for Scott and Ed.

"Are you trying to get yourselves killed?" Scott shouted angrily as he paced back and forth in front of them."

"They looked human. We couldn't tell the difference," Ben stated.

"Ten days. They reminded us about the deadline."

Ed stood up. "I'm going to let John and the Anunnaki know." He turned and pointed a finger at Logan, "But you, mister, had better listen to your father.

"I know. I'm sorry. It was a mistake. I don't ever want to see those guys again."

"Me, neither!" agreed Ben.

"But you know what, there's a mystery. I would really like to know how that girl knew that those guys were Cioth." He turned to Ed, "You know who I mean, the girl who gave you her bike."

"Yeah, me too," added Ben. "She pointed them out! Hey, wait, she gave you her bike?"

Ed waved a dismissive hand, "She was trying to be nice, that's all. She had just collided with Logan. And, think about it, how could she possibly know anything about the Cioth?"

Ben shrugged, "I don't know, but before she took off, she said, 'It's them.' She knew!"

"I think you should forget it. She couldn't possibly know. She probably just got lucky, or maybe unlucky in your case." Ed dropped his head as if contemplating something. When he looked up again, he glanced briefly at Ben, "You said they resembled each other; that's probably why she noticed them."

Logan suddenly poked a finger into the air. "Wait, I'm s-o-o stupid. We've got a picture!" He called up the image on his phone and passed it to his dad.

"Okay, well, this changes things," Scott sounded pleased. "This is really useful. We can keep an eye out for them now."

"Nice work boys," said Ed. "You paid the price, but you got something valuable."

"I still think it was too high a price," Scott was patting Logan on the back. "You've both had enough for today. Ben, you look beat up, and Logan, you have a nasty burn that you have to take care of. I want the two of you to take it easy tonight. Why don't you get something to eat and try to relax? I want to know where you are, because Ed and I have too much to do to be worried about you."

Ed was shaking his head. "Not me, I'm going back to the island. I have some things to pick up, and now I have something to pass on about the Cioth." He smiled, "So don't wait up!"

"It looks like you've been working really hard, so, how's it going?" Logan asked, happy to change the subject.

"Pretty good," Scott gave his son a weak smile, "It won't matter much though, if the Anunnaki don't find the antidote."

Ed nodded, "I'll let you know how they're doing on that front, when I get back. Right now, I need a change of clothes, and I think I'll take that jacket of yours, Scott. Let me know if you think of anything else we need before I leave." Ed headed for the stairs to the guest room.

"We need more food!" Logan yelled after him.

"Yeah, more of those pancake things and some more green milk," Ben called out, as he finished off his drink.

"Right!" Ed shouted back, "So you like those, do you? Don't worry. I won't forget."

When Ed returned to the garage, he was wearing one of Scott's hats and a heavy red shirt under Scott's blue jacket. Everyone stared at him because something had changed.

"You shaved!" Scott was the first to realize.

"Yes!" said Logan, pointing at Ed. "Who is this guy?" He began to walk back and forth inspecting the change. Finally, he folded his arms and broke into a broad smile. "You look so different. I've never seen you without your moustache and beard."

"Yeah," Ben agreed, "You really don't look like you anymore."

"Are you sure it's dark enough out to leave?" Scott asked. "Someone might see you."

"Didn't you hear them?" Ed jerked his thumb at the boys, "I don't look like me. Don't worry. I'll be careful."

"Okay, I just don't want anything to happen. I need your help." Scott patted Ed on the back and said, "By the way, if you can manage it, I wouldn't mind some of those Anunnaki drinks. They help me to stay awake, and they don't get me wired like coffee."

"Will do," Ed said, as he swung his backpack over his shoulder. "I'll see you boys in the morning. Sleep tight."

Scott walked Ed to the door and watched him leave.

"How is he getting to the marina?" asked Logan, "Aren't you going to drive him?"

"Don't have to. I rented him a car. It's the blue one out front. I figured people might take a second look if they saw a stranger driving my car. Besides that, there should always be one of us here, working, or we'll never get done on time."

Ben and Logan finished off the last of the Anunnaki pancakes and took Darth out for a walk. "I don't think they'd try anything when we have Darth with us, do you?" asked Ben.

Logan had been thinking the same thing. "I doubt it," Logan agreed, but the truth was, he wasn't at all sure. He didn't want to find out, either.

* * *

Since they were both too excited after their encounter with the Cioth to settle down, they spent the rest of the evening doing whatever they could to help Scott. Logan barely recognized the garage. There were boxes of stuff stacked against the garage door and two worktables pushed together in the middle of the room. There were new IKEA halogen pole lamps. The boys help to set them up near the tables and Logan noticed that his father had brought the coffee machine in from the kitchen. Scott hardly looked up from his work and only then to point at something that needed to be done. Around midnight, he sent everybody to bed.

Darth followed them upstairs and sat and watched while Logan smeared the burn ointment all over his face and neck. Perhaps the dog sensed something, because he jumped onto the bed and curled up next to Logan, something he'd never done before. Things were different now and even leaving the light on in the hallway seemed like a good idea.

CHAPTER 45

THE NEXT MORNING, LOGAN AWOKE to an uncomfortable feeling. His eyes weren't even open yet when he knew something was wrong. His skin felt funny, like it had been stretched too tight across his face.

"Hey, Ben, are you awake?" Logan asked in a loud whisper.

Ben was curled up on a cot on the other side of the room. All Logan could see was Ben's dark hair sticking out from the blankets. He wasn't stirring.

Logan crawled out of bed and made his way to the bathroom across the hall. He leaned over the sink and peered at himself in the mirror. "Wow," he muttered. His face was a bright red.

He jogged downstairs in search of his father, but after finding the garage empty, and no Ed around either, he returned upstairs.

Back in his parents' room, Logan found his father lying across the bed, completely buried under a comforter. He looked unconscious, so there was no way he was going to wake him, even if he could.

Back in his own room Logan began to shake Ben, "Wake up, come on Ben, I need you to get up!"

Without even opening his eyes, Ben pulled the covers over his head. "Later, okay?" he moaned.

This whole time Darth had been following Logan from room to room.

"Great. You probably need to go out, right?"

Darth's tail began to thrash back and forth, and he dashed into the hall to wait at the top of the stairs.

Logan wasn't sure what to do. He went back to the bathroom, smeared the ointment that the doctor had given him, all over his face. He found an old baseball hat in the hall closet and jammed it onto his head, pulling the visor down as far as it would go. He led the dog through the kitchen, but when he opened the back door, Darth sat down and stared up at Logan. "Look, you'll get your usual walk later; I just need you to go out back for now, okay buddy?"

After much coaxing, Darth lowered his head and walked out onto the back deck. "Sorry pal, I can't help it, my face looks like I belong in a horror movie and I don't feel so good right now."

Several minutes later, as he was checking on Darth, Logan was shocked to see Mr. Einhorn, leaning over the fence into their yard. *What's this?* Logan wondered as he watched the nosy neighbour trying to talk to his dog. Logan was just about to open the door and call for Darth, when Ben came up behind him, giving him a start.

"Nice sunburn!" Ben observed.

CHAPTER 46

DEEFIN AND THREE OTHERS FOLLOWED the long winding passage to a particular door. The lighting in this room was always dim, because this was what the specimens in this room required: they lived in darkness, always scurrying from the light. The transfer would occur here.

Deep below Wolf Island, the mood had changed, particularly for one of the Anunnaki. Deefin, for his part, saw that the Cioth were becoming more destructive and balked at the Anunnaki's policy of non-interference.

From the beginning, the Cioth had lied about their intentions, that all they wanted was the sphere, that the Earth held nothing else of interest for them. In secret, they had already begun to pillage the planet, taking grain, animals and precious minerals. They had amassed their treasures at key collection points around the globe and were preparing to shuttle them to the Cioth ships high in orbit above the Earth and on to the Cioth home world.

In response, the Anunnaki had formulated a plan to disrupt the murderous Cioth's activities, while they continued to search for an antidote to the sleeping poison. Within hours, the Anunnaki had seeded their cargo at one Cioth collection point, and remained to watch the Cioth ships depart.

Aboard one Cioth ship high in Earth orbit, two crewmembers sat at a large computer terminal—their job was to log each container as it arrived. One container was not labelled in any way and this prompted an investigation. Other crewmembers were summoned for assistance. The lid to the container gave them a little trouble, and for some reason, the lock mechanism was unfamiliar. With a bit of effort though, they pried the lid open and peered into the darkness.

In seconds, dozens of black, spider-like creatures spilled into the room. The Crootta and her offspring had emerged, and did what the Crootta does: eat every living thing.

The ship was programmed to return to the Cioth home world. There would be thousands of Crootta by the time the ship landed on the Cioth home world. At least, that was the plan.

CHAPTER 47

They followed the voices to the garage. Scott and Ed were awake and hard at it. Ed had evidently already returned from Wolf Island.

"You guys okay?" Scott asked glancing up at Logan's red face. "Hope you're still putting on that ointment."

"Yup, I am. Well, what did the Anunnaki say about the cure?" Logan asked anxiously.

Ed was sitting in front of a control panel, which looked worthy of anything NASA could devise. Turning his chair in their direction, they could see that he was frowning. "I'm sorry, guys, they're still working on it. I was just telling your father that the Anunnaki say they need some blood from an infected person."

"My parents!" Ben interrupted. "We could get some from one of my parents. I know they would volunteer, if they...," his voice trailed off.

"Well, that's really nice of you Ben, but we're actually thinking about Logan's mother. I'm taking Ed over there to visit her later. He was a medic when he was in the Navy, so he knows how to do it. We'll just have to hope that no one recognizes him."

"I'm pretty sure that no one will," Logan remarked.

"By the way, we're ready for the test," Scott beamed. "My father's machine, at least our part, is over there on the work bench. We'll be standing over here." He was standing in front of a table with a large workstation and screen. "If you're staying, you'll both have to put on a pair of these safety glasses," he said, gesturing at another table. "You can never be too safe, right Logan?"

"Yup," Logan nodded absently as he leaned over his father's shoulder and stared at the computer screen.

Ed's control panel was lit up with different coloured lights that were blinking in unison. "You know," he said glancing up, "I think I'd feel better if we all put on some ear protection as well. It's entirely possible, that this thing might be capable of putting out some high decibels."

The group hunted around until everyone was wearing both eye and ear protection.

"It won't explode, will it?" Ben joked.

"I really hope not!" Ed said, his eyes locked on the computer display.

Ben took three steps back.

"Ready?" Scott asked, glancing at Ed.

"Ready."

Scott held up crossed fingers to the boys.

"Good luck, Dad," said Logan.

"I'm just going to apply half power now, then we'll slowly bump it up."

"How will we know if it worked?" Ben asked just as Scott called out, "Now!"

Nothing happened. No lights, not a sound.

"What's supposed to happen?" Ben asked. "Is that it?"

Logan waved to get Ben's attention and held a finger to his lips.

Ed placed a hand on Scott's shoulder.

Scott sat motionless in his chair, both hands resting on the table in front of him. He stared at his work. A wisp of smoke rose from the workbench. To his mind, something here didn't add up. *Could this device, this machine, the way it's designed, be right?*

He sighed deeply and rubbed his eyes. Feeling discouraged, but realizing that there was only one way forward, Scott leaned over and re-booted his computer. No matter what, he would figure this out, he'd find out what went wrong and he'd fix it.

"Well, I guess we do what we have to do," Ed got to his feet, "but coffee first."

Scott nodded at the suggestion, "You realize that this would be a lot easier if we had a decent power source and scientific equipment that could measure our results."

"I do," Ed agreed as they left the room.

The wisp of smoke still lingered in the air. It was a vital clue that was missed at the time, a subtle effect that could not be measured.

Alone now, Scott stared at the coil, the one that Cathy had gone to pick up. It glistened in the light. It seemed to him that the coil was at the centre of it all, but what was its purpose? Something about its size put it out of context. The machine resembled something much larger, but he couldn't quite put his finger on it. Still, he needed a break and there was something that he, that all of them had to do.

CHAPTER 48

THE HOSPITAL WAS CROWDED. EVEN with the local health department and the Center for Disease Control checking everything—water, air and food—people were still getting sick. Bringing in food from the city hadn't helped either. Eventually the specialists concluded that the food was being tampered with once it arrived in Milford. Now the authorities were looking for a lunatic or terrorists.

The citizens of Milford were told not to buy anything sold locally. Get your food from the trucks bringing in the food and take it directly home, they were advised. In response, the Cioth grew impatient and began to put their poison directly into the town's drinking water, the same water that the CDC had declared safe and free from any foreign agent—it never occurred to anyone that checking the water *once* wasn't enough! The problem was growing. No one was safe.

Scott and Ed arrived at Cathy's bedside about the same time that Ben and Logan arrived at the bedsides of Ben's parents for a brief visit. In a leather pouch, Ed carried a needle and glass vial for taking blood. The Anunnaki had told him that only one vial would be necessary for their analysis, but they needed it as soon as possible. With Scott standing on guard, Ed inserted the needle into a vein in Cathy's arm and drew out enough blood to fill the vial. Cathy didn't stir. Scott leaned over and whispered into his wife's ear. "Your blood is going to help us find a cure, Cathy. I'll be back to see you as soon as I can."

"Excuse me, gentlemen. What are you doing there? Visiting hours are over," a harried nurse called out from the nurses' station.

"We were just visiting my wife." Scott called out to her. "We're leaving now." The two men hustled down the corridor to find Ben and Logan.

Back home, Ed unbuckled the pouch containing the vial and placed it on the kitchen counter. The weather had been getting worse all day, and it was expected to last most of the night. Heavy wind and rain were making visibility poor. It was not a good time to return to the island. Ed decided that he had no choice but to wait it out and leave the first thing next morning.

CHAPTER 49

ABOARD THE *DISCO VOLANTE*, THEY cleared the harbour channel, and Ed throttled up the big boat's twin engines. It was a perfect day to be out on the water: the temperature was mild, the sun was shining, and the water was calm with hardly a ripple.

Darth had jumped into the passenger seat beside Ed, and it was obvious that nothing was going to move him. Logan and Ben laughed as they took their seats at the back of the boat. They felt a little better and were quite happy to stretch out their legs, lean back, and let the wind whip at their faces and hair.

It only occurred to the boys after arriving off the island that they had not passed a single boat. At that time of year, there should have been boats of all types criss-crossing the lake, from catamarans to cabin cruisers, jet skis, kayaks and paddleboards. It was eerie but understandable. Earlier that day, they had heard on the car radio that the town council had voted unanimously, citing safety concerns, to cancel the annual corn roast. Logan couldn't ever remember a time when there wasn't a corn roast to mark the end of summer.

Ed moored the boat just off shore, mindful of the giant rocks just beneath the surface. He held onto Darth as Logan and Ben lowered themselves over the side into the water. The rocks were slippery, so the boys held onto the boat and guided it to shore.

Ed was the last one in the boat. He tossed two knapsacks to the boys and climbed over the side. On the beach, Logan and Ben were helping each other with the knapsacks when they heard a cry and looked up. There was Ed, face down in the water, struggling to get up.

The teens dropped the knapsacks and plunged headlong into the water. They grabbed Ed by the arms and dragged him out of the water.

Ed began to curse. He was holding his stomach. His shirt was covered in blood.

CHAPTER 50

John McCarthy and one of the Anunnaki were waiting just inside the tunnel when the boys arrived. Logan assumed that this alien must be Deefin. For some reason, he seemed to be everywhere his grandfather was.

Darth had been just behind the boys. Now he came bounding out of the bushes straight at John almost knocking him to the ground. Deefin was watching closely as John talked and stroked the dog. The alien began to pace nervously as Darth began to dance around him and his old master.

John spotted Ed struggling down the hill, into the crater. He was favouring one leg that seemed to be slowing him down and causing him more than a little discomfort. As soon as the alien spotted Ed's blood-soaked shirt, he gasped. Ed smiled and stepped closer, holding up his hands. "Not my blood, Deefin," he said. "It's not mine. I'm okay."

Despite Ed's assurances, Deefin remained wide-eyed, wringing his hands nervously. Not knowing what else to do, Ed pulled up his shirt to show Deefin his chest. "See?" he said, smiling. "Just a scratch!"

"Thank heaven you're not hurt," John said, trying to calm Deefin, but coming to a grim conclusion: "…. if it's not your blood, is it the sample we've been waiting for?"

Ed dropped his head and rubbed his forehead. It was a nervous habit that John knew too well. It confirmed his worst suspicions. The vial was broken. The blood was lost.

"I'm so sorry. I'm afraid I slipped on those damn rocks getting out of the boat," Ed confessed. "I don't know what to say."

John stepped over to his friend. "Nothing," he said, as he relieved Ed of his backpack. "It's not your fault. I've had a few slips on those rocks myself over the years. We'll just have to get another sample."

"Ben and I are going back right away," Logan said. "Maybe Dad can get another sample, and we promise to bring it right over."

"No, that's not going to work," growled Ed. "This is up to me. Besides, your father doesn't know how to take blood."

Logan pointed at Ed's foot, "You can hardly walk. Ben and I can go faster without you."

"Wait a minute!" John was holding up his hands for quiet. "Before we decide anything, there are some things I need you to take back to your dad." He was staring at Logan. "And you, Ed, I don't know where you think you're going with that leg. Let's take a look at it!"

"I think…" Ed started to say.

"Needs fluids," said a voice from behind.

"What?" Ben asked, looking around.

"Needs fluids now."

Everyone turned to Deefin. He was staring down at Darth. "This animal," Deefin said, "it needs fluids."

"You're right," John agreed. "He could probably use a drink of water."

An hour later, with the backpacks now filled with food, John was putting pages of notes into a watertight container. "These are for your dad," he explained. "They should help with his problem."

"As far as the blood sample is concerned, I think our only option is for the three of you to go back together. Ed is right. Your dad doesn't know how to draw blood, and Ed looks okay to me."

"Before you leave," John whispered to Logan, "I need to give you something." He turned his back to the others before pulling something small from his pocket. He handed Logan what looked like a silver computer mouse. Logan was about to examine it, when his grandfather nudged his hand. "Put it in your pocket, I want you to have this in case you run into the Cioth again."

"What is it?" Logan asked, as he ran his fingers over the object's smooth surface in his pocket.

"It's a kind of tranquilizer gun," explained John. "And believe me when I tell you to be extremely careful with it. The Anunnaki use these to knock out only the largest and most aggressive animals. One shot from this thing can take down a buffalo. So please be careful, and if you need to use it, only use it on the Cioth."

"So how do I...?" began Logan.

"All you have to do is aim and press the button on top twice, holding it down the second time. The first press arms the weapon and the second press is the shot. Got that?"

Logan nodded, "Got it."

"By the way, even if someone else got their hands on it, they wouldn't be able to use it. I've programmed it for your DNA."

Logan nodded again, "Thanks, Grampa."

It took three trips to the surface, first Logan and Ben with the loaded backpacks, then Ed, leaning heavily against John, Deefin carrying a long black case for the water tight container, and finally two Anunnaki with a piece of equipment.

At the mouth of the tunnel, the Anunnaki stopped to unfold a somewhat uncomfortable looking stretcher for Ed. The webbing resembled dull grey strips of steel, and one look had Ben feeling sorry for Ed. This could be a very long and uncomfortable ride back to the boat.

With a little persuasion from John, Ed finally approached the waiting stretcher. "I find this embarrassing," he protested. "I could probably make it if I had a crutch." After looking from person to person and finding no agreement, he finally lay down on the stretcher. A surprised look was followed by a smile, "Ooh, not bad!"

Ben watched as both the Anunnaki donned a harness that would allow them to carry the stretcher while leaving their hands free.

It was already twilight, and Logan was getting anxious to leave. At last, he led the group away from the tunnel.

"It's okay. Go on," he heard his grandfather say behind him.

Logan turned to see who his grandfather was talking to.

"Not you Logan. It's Darth. He's not moving. I think you'd better call him," his grandfather said. "He can't stay here."

Both boys watched as Darth flopped down in front of John. Logan noticed that the dog's eyes were wide open and darting around. He looked afraid.

Darth struggled to his feet. He threw his mouth open and retched. His stomach heaved, and vomit shot from his mouth. Barely able to keep himself upright, his legs collapsed under him. He sank to the ground, closed his eyes, and began to whimper.

Ed struggled to get off the stretcher, and John and the boys knelt down, trying to comfort the dog. The Anunnaki exchanged glances. In unison, they turned their attention to John. Some communication must have passed from the Anunnaki to their human friends, because John and Ed appeared to be considering something.

"Logan," he began, "the Anunnaki believe that Darth has been poisoned. You've probably realized that yourself. They're saying it has to be the same poison that the humans have ingested, so they would like to analyze the dog's vomit, and they'll need some of his blood."

Ed had his hand on Logan's shoulder for support. "I hate to say it, but it makes perfect sense. The Anunnaki can take the blood sample from Darth, and I promise they'll take care of him." Ed was reassuring himself as much as the others. "Hurry everyone, let's get him off the ground and make him comfortable. We can put him on the stretcher. I won't need it after all. I'm staying here tonight."

Logan and Ben were still on the ground next to Darth. They were patting him, trying to hold back their tears. "We're going to stay with him, too."

Darth had already slipped into a coma by the time the Anunnaki placed him on the stretcher and extracted a small vial of blood.

"They won't let anything happen to him. I promise you that," John told the boys in a firm voice. "But I'm afraid I have to ask you to return home tonight." He turned to Logan, who was frowning. "I really am sorry, but your father is going to be really worried, and besides, he'll need the papers I've prepared for him as soon as possible. If you like, I can have the Anunnaki accompany you to the boat."

Logan and Ben insisted on getting back to the boat on their own. The walk was quiet, with both boys lost in their own thoughts, and neither of them spoke a word until they arrived back at the house.

Scott had been making coffee and was about to grab a snack when the boys came in. After seeing their faces, he knew something had happened. "Where's Ed… and where's Darth?"

CHAPTER 51

WHEN LOGAN CAME DOWNSTAIRS THE next morning, he could hear Ben talking to his dad in the kitchen. "Do you really think your dad's machine is going to work now?" Ben asked.

"I sure hope so," Scott told him, "And once this whole thing is behind us, we have to make sure that nothing like this can ever happen again. We have to make sure the Cioth never return."

Scott had turned on the coffee machine, and now the noise was drowning out Ben's voice, but Logan could just make out something about Darth, the poison and how he'd like to murder the Cioth.

"What's up?" Logan asked as he rounded the corner into the kitchen.

"Nothing," said Ben, "we were just talking."

"I thought I heard you say that you want to murder the Cioth, but you can wait in line."

Scott was pouring his coffee when he interrupted the boys. "What have you guys got planned for today? I'm thinking I'd rather have you close to home."

Ben had climbed onto one of the bar stools beside the counter. He was holding a plastic bag. Logan recognized it as one of the four that they had brought home with them the night before. The food inside was a dull blue colour.

"It tastes better than it looks." Scott smiled, seeing Logan's expression, "You should know that by now."

Ben looked sideways at Scott as he pulled some small blue nuggets out of the bag. When he opened his hand for a closer look, he realized that they resembled tiny pineapples. "I know we should be grateful that everything the Anunnaki send us tastes a lot better than it looks. I just wish they weren't these ugly colours."

Logan dropped onto the stool next to Ben, and scooped up the plastic bag. "I know it tastes pretty good, but I miss bacon and eggs."

Ben popped a few of the blue nuggets into his mouth. "Ahh," he smiled as he rubbed his stomach, "delicious, breakfast of champions!"

"Idiot!" Logan was shaking his head as he pushed Ben away. "I know you'd kill for bacon and eggs."

"I might," Ben laughed. "By the way, I want to go over to my house today. I won't take long. I just need a change of clothes."

Scott stared at Ben for a moment. "Yeah, okay, but I don't want you to go by yourself. I think Logan should go with you. It would make me happy to have you here with me, or at the very least, in public places."

"Public places are empty now, Dad," Logan pointed out.

"Yeah, I guess you're right," his father frowned, "but please be aware of your surroundings, and call me every hour. It's hard to work when I'm worried."

"Remember, the Anunnaki won't let the Cioth kill anyone. Isn't that right? So, as long as we don't eat anything, we'll be fine," reasoned Ben. "Anyway, they already had a chance to kill us and they didn't."

A short time later, the boys headed to the back door. For the second time, Logan was surprised to see his neighbour, Mr. Einhorn, leaning over the fence. He was looking for something. He straightened up as soon as he saw Logan and Ben at the door.

"Hi there," he greeted them. "I'm glad to see you both still healthy."

Hmm, thought Logan, *for a man who doesn't like teenagers and us in particular, this seems like an unusually cheerful greeting.* The boys ignored him and kept walking.

"I haven't seen Darth today," said Mr. Einhorn, looking around. "Don't you always take him for a walk about now? Nothing wrong with him I hope."

Logan had nearly crossed the yard, but now he stopped and spun around to face his neighbour. "OH NO, it was you!" he shouted. "You poisoned my dog, didn't you!"

"I don't know what you're talking about!" Einhorn began to edge away from the fence.

"I know it was you! I saw you out here a few days ago, hanging over the fence, like today! You were feeding him." Why would you do that, what's he ever done to you?"

Einhorn's face went from innocent to guilty to angry in a second. "This whole thing is your family's fault, all these people getting sick. It's your father's fault!"

Ben jabbed an accusing finger at Einhorn. "You're crazy. You don't even know what you're talking about."

"I know darn well that your father brought something alien back with him from Africa. Something so terrible, so lethal, it's making everyone in this town sick. It's probably airborne, and God only knows where it will stop!"

"Wow, you're nuts!" Logan shouted. "My parents didn't bring anything back with them."

Ben nodded and started to pull his friend back. "Listen Logan, we don't have time to talk to this guy. We should go." Over his shoulder, Ben shouted back at Einhorn, "You'd better hope Darth is okay!" and extended his middle finger.

It was a futile gesture. Einhorn smirked and walked away.

"He'll be sorry," Logan grumbled. He was still extremely angry and staring after Mr. Einhorn when Ben shoved an empty backpack toward him.

"Forget him. He'll get his," Ben said as he retrieved his bike from against the house.

The ride to Ben's house only took ten minutes.

They propped their bikes against the garage door, opened the gate and followed the brick path around to the back of the house. Ben stared down now at the long grass.

Logan had been watching him from the deck. "I know how you feel."

No sooner did they open the door when a strong, foul smell hit them in the face. Logan waved his hand in front of his face, "Oh, man," he groaned, "what is that? It's gross!"

"Oh! It must be the fish!" Ben held his nose and pulled out a plastic garbage bag from under the sink.

Logan stepped aside as Ben made a dash for the door. Even just holding the bag was making Ben gag. He swung the bag out the door and threw it as far as he could away from the house.

"Wow!" said Logan, puffing out a big breath. "That was the worst thing I've ever smelled!"

"You can say that again," agreed Ben. "They got sick right after dinner, so the garbage wasn't taken out and... I'll just get my stuff."

Logan followed his friend up the stairs to his room.

Ben started pulling things out of his drawers. He tossed an armful to Logan, who shoved everything into a backpack.

"Okay," Ben said, "I just need to get my toothbrush."

As he headed toward the bathroom, he realized that something was wrong. The buzzing had started. He grabbed his toothbrush and returned to the bedroom, where Logan was slipping on one of the backpacks. Ben grabbed the other pack and put it on.

"Let's get out of here," Ben could feel himself starting to sweat a little as he headed for the stairs.

The buzzing increased, faster than ever before. At the top of the stairs, he stopped to peer over the railing. Logan was about to go around him, when Ben put out his arm. "I think I just heard something," he whispered.

The boys watched as two shadows appeared in the hall below. Ben motioned for Logan to follow him to the window in his room.

They had removed the screen and were fumbling with the lock on the window when they heard a familiar sound. They spun around to find two figures standing mere steps away in the hall. Cioth!

Logan felt a panic begin to consume him. He had to think, there must be something they could do. Some way to stop these…*The tranquilizer!* The weapon Grampa had given him. *Yes,* he thought as he began to pat his jacket pockets. *Nothing!*

The aliens had stopped, they were relishing the fear they were reading on the boys' faces.

Ben froze. Logan dragged his friend to the far side of the bed. He dug both hands into his pants pockets and found what he was searching for, just as the aliens surged forward.

The weapon made no sound at all. A silvery blast of plasma shot across the room, spreading wider as it moved. With tremendous force, it struck the aliens, throwing them back against the far wall. An opaque mist obscured the creatures where they fell.

Ben and Logan huddled against the window.

As the silvery mist slowly started to dissipate, the boys watched in terror as both aliens drew forward.

"Crap, Crap!" Logan yelled, as he raised the weapon again and fired, pressing down twice as instructed, holding the button hard and long.

Ben had one hand on Logan's shoulder, his legs were trembling and the buzzing in his head was unbearable.

Again, the silvery blast of plasma knocked the creatures back against the wall, enveloping them in mist. Seconds passed. Again, the mist evaporated, revealing the aliens relentlessly advancing on their position.

"They're still coming!" Ben shrieked.

"DIE! DIE!" screamed Logan as he pressed the button repeatedly, his fingers white with the pressure.

The mist was taking longer to clear this time. Logan grabbed Ben by the arm and began to drag him toward the door. As the boys fled by the cloud, a hand reached out and grabbed Logan by the leg. Logan stumbled backwards, hit his head on the closet door and dropped the weapon. His vision faded to black.

Ben could hardly breathe. He collapsed on the floor near Logan, and for a scant second, he couldn't make sense of what happened. In a daze, he raised his head enough to see the creature begin to drag Logan closer.

They were alone and no one was coming to their rescue. He had to do something to help Logan. He needed to find the weapon. Where was it, where did it go?

Ben spotted the second alien, a weapon in his hand. His heart sank. The creature aimed at Logan.

"No!" Ben yelled as he held up his hand to the Cioth. The buzzing in his head seemed to radiate down his arm. He could feel it leaving his body as a dazzling, white light shot out from his fingertips. It struck the alien with tremendous force, and lifted him into the air. Blackness. A puff of air struck Ben in the face.

Ben jerked up. He felt stunned. *What was that?* He stared down at his hands in disbelief, then wonder.

The Cioth who had been holding onto Logan was gone.

"Good!" Ben yelled, relieved. *But where was the other one, the one that had been hit by the white light?* On the other side of the bed, a small pile of white dust lay on the floor. Ben kicked his foot through it. It looked like ash.

It was ten minutes before Logan opened his eyes. Ben gave him a hand and helped him up.

"Where are they?" Logan asked as he rubbed his forehead. "What happened?"

"Um, I guess your tranquilizer gun worked," Ben lied. "They're gone." He gazed at the pile of dust and shivered. *Who or what am I?*

CHAPTER 52

DAN PACKARD SAT IN FRONT of the computer monitor in his cubicle. For ten years, it had been his job to study satellite images from various locations along the east coast. A week before, something had grabbed his attention, something that he had to think about for a few days before deciding to take a chance. In the end, he'd ordered closer surveillance on a particular area, a place he thought of as a hot spot. Wolf Island had been the whispered topic of speculation around the office for the past year. He had heard some strange stories on the job, but the ones connected with the island had gotten pretty weird, unreal.

When the video footage arrived, he was nervous to see what surveillance might have picked up. *Please*, he thought to himself, *let there be something I can show the boss*.

After studying the images, and zooming in as close as possible, Dan stared in disbelief. What he was looking at on the screen simply couldn't be, yet there it was. He took a deep breath and snatched up the phone.

"Vanderholt," a voice answered immediately.

"Yes, sir, this is Dan Packard, section one."

"Right. Have you got something for me?"

"I think I might," answered Dan. "I need you to take a look at something."

"Be right there," Henry Vanderholt replied. He took a big gulp of his cold coffee and got up. Henry had never been a patient man. He supervised over 100 people and rarely had time for lunch, or anything else for that matter. Staff members were reluctant to trouble him.

Arriving at Packard's cubicle, Henry leaned on the desk. "So, what have you got for me?"

Dan brought up the satellite image from a week before. "I noticed this boat going back and forth between Wolf Island and that marina. It's made several trips."

Henry looked irritated. "Haven't you heard that they have some kind of plague or something over there? The CDC thinks it might be a lunatic who is poisoning food. The guys in that boat were probably fishing. It makes sense that they were trying to get something safe to eat." He grumbled as he turned to leave."

"Wait, just one moment, sir." Dan brought up a new screen, a close-up of the beach and the occupants of the boat. Vanderholt watched as the recording showed two teenage boys helping an older man onto his feet. He appeared to have fallen.

Dan zoomed in on the older man's face, closer and closer, until it filled the screen. "Now look," he said as he turned his chair, and pointed at a picture that had been taped to the wall. Both men stared at the picture and back at the screen several times.

"Holy… It can't be," said Henry. "That's impossible!"

CHAPTER 53

The boys spotted the van from down the street. The occupants had parked it halfway between the Einhorn property and his parents' house. Logan watched as two men and a woman exited the van and walked over to talk to Mr. Einhorn, who seemed to be expecting them.

Einhorn had both arms around his rake, pulling it to his chest, striking an amiable, neighbourly pose. After a few moments, he leaned in closer as if he were sharing a secret, but jerked his head toward Logan's house.

Logan and Ben wheeled into the driveway and jumped off their bikes, dropping them onto the lawn. "Are you going to tell your father about the aliens?" Ben asked in a voice just above a whisper.

"Um- I don't think so," Logan shook his head, "If we do, he'll never let us out of the house again. Besides, he has enough to worry about, like for instance, what old Einhorn is up to." He jabbed his thumb toward the neighbour's house.

From inside the house, the boys watched the three people open the back of the van and don white masks and suits.

"Uh, oh," Ben huffed, "Those are hazmat suits, I think we know what Mr. Einhorn has been saying."

"Dad, we've got company!" Logan yelled as he watched the trio walk up the path to their door.

Scott came rushing into the hallway at the same moment the doorbell rang.

Logan made no move for the door. "Dad," he whispered, "Mr. Einhorn has been saying that we're the ones who've been poisoning everyone. You know, because of your trip."

Scott raised his eyebrows and stared at his son for a moment. When he opened the door, he found three people wearing hazmat suits and masks. One of them had a folder that he held up for Scott.

"What's all this about?" asked Scott, pretending not to have a clue. "Please don't tell me that my neighbour has been telling wild stories again."

A look and a frown passed briefly between the three inspectors.

"Ahh, I thought as much," Scott rolled his eyes in disgust. "Well look, if there's anything I can do, I'm more than happy to help. I heard on the news that the police think some crazy person is going around poisoning people, so obviously, you have to do your job and follow every lead. I have to tell you that I'm terribly distressed about all this because my wife and my friends are in the hospital."

"We're very sorry about this sir," the woman said. "We've received a tip, and we have to follow up. This means we have to search your house."

"Yes, of course, I thought as much," Scott said, as he stepped away from the door and motioned them inside.

"Please, help yourselves. I'll be in the garage if you have any questions."

It took two hours to search the McCarthy house. This was mainly due to the many questions about the fascinating work going on in the garage. Scott made his answers so complicated that nobody could possibly understand a word of it. The three health inspectors smiled and nodded, but were clueless.

At the door, Scott pointed out that no one from next door had been poisoned; in fact, they seemed to be going about their business, completely unconcerned. And just lately, Mr. Einhorn was seen dropping food over the fence onto this property and shortly thereafter, the family dog got sick. Perhaps the guilty party is trying to point the finger elsewhere?

Logan and Ben had been sitting quietly during the search. Now they were crouched below the window in the living room, watching the inspectors head next door.

"Boys, I have a favour to ask." Scott had a serious expression. "I'm not sure if those health inspectors will be back, so I want you to go over to the professor's house and ask him to meet Ed's boat and keep him at his house for awhile." He held up his hand before the boys could point out a serious problem with the plan. "I know the professor thinks that Ed and your grandfather are dead, but just think how relieved he'll be when he finds out the truth."

CHAPTER 54

A FEW HOURS LATER, MR. Einhorn slammed his front door as the health inspectors left.

"How dare they send those people over here! I know it was them," bellowed Einhorn. "They'll pay for this, we're the innocent ones. They're the problem. You know we were just trying to be helpful." Daryl Einhorn had been ranting ever since he'd answered the door to the inspectors. An hour later, he was still at it, and it didn't look as though he planned to stop anytime soon.

Ivy had had enough. She dropped onto the sofa and crossed her arms. "For heaven's sake, Daryl, shut up! You're giving me a headache."

Utter shock crossed Einhorn's face. He was speechless. In all their years together, Ivy had never talked to him like this. In fact, she had always agreed with everything he'd said and done. Daryl's eyes bulged as he stared at her for a minute. Who exactly did she think she was?' Why was she talking to him like this all of a sudden? Well, he simply couldn't allow it.

"You started it, you accused him first," Ivy went on. "In fact, you're always accusing someone of something, even me, and I'm sick of it. I'm not going to stand for it any longer."

Daryl had been sitting in his easy chair, but then he sprang up and loomed over his wife. "Why you ungrateful woman, how dare you!" His face was turning red. "After all I've done for you. You wouldn't live in a nice house like this, if it weren't for me. You would never have had a nice job, if I hadn't helped you. You are the most …"

He brought his foot back, Ivy braced herself for a kick, but instead the coffee table flew past her and knocked the lamp over. He was out of control, angry, and yelling. Ivy sat there and pretended that she couldn't hear. "That's it, that's it," he shouted as spit flew out of his mouth. "I've had enough." He stomped from the room.

"So have I," Ivy murmured.

It was 2:00 o'clock in the morning when the stairs creaked under the weight of something heavy. Ivy knew who it was, but she didn't care, she just rolled over and went back to sleep.

Daryl brought a number of blue plastic containers from the basement, up to the kitchen where he filled them with all the canned food in the house. It took him another hour to haul the containers along with bottled water and a number of blankets down to their bomb shelter. No one would ever find him there, unless it was his idea: the shelter was extremely well hidden, and only he and Ivy knew of its existence and location in the house. Einhorn's father had always kept it well stocked, and when Daryl took over the house, he'd done the same. He knew it already contained enough food to sustain him for several months, but up until now, he had refused to touch it.

Let her try to get along without me, he thought. *She'll be sorry and come banging on the door. I think I might even ignore her after the way she talked to me.*

"Serves you right!" he yelled as he banged the door shut and bolted it from the inside.

It was morning when Einhorn had second thoughts and attempted to open the door. It wouldn't budge. He had no way of knowing that his wife had blocked the door and would never return.

CHAPTER 55

IT WAS LATER IN THE day when the boys headed over to the Prentiss house. The shadows were long and there was a slight breeze off the lake. Ordinarily, there would be people out and about, enjoying the perfect weather. Now, Milford was a ghost town, where only people in hazard suits roamed the streets.

Professor Prentiss was at home and looking very tired. These days he could only be found in one of two places, the hospital or home. School wasn't due to open for another three weeks, but the professor knew that if the poisonings didn't stop, perhaps it never would. He shuffled his way to the door. He had lost weight, and he hadn't shaved in days. He knew that it looked like he'd been sleeping in his clothes, which was true. When he opened the door to the boys, he couldn't even muster a smile. He simply stared at them until they told him that Logan's father needed a favour, and that it was an emergency.

The professor didn't say a word, as Logan and Ben told him as much as they thought would convince him to help. They were not even sure that he understood what they were saying. At the mention of his old friend, John McCarthy, the boys noticed a change: the professor's eyes were now wide open. A flash of guilt crossed his face. "How soon do you think Ed will be getting to the marina?" he now asked.

"Any time now," Logan replied, relieved and anxious at the same time. "Ed said he would be coming over today, but I'm not sure what time. I think I should tell you, when you get there, you might not recognize him at first, he shaved off his beard and his moustache."

"That's right," agreed Ben, smiling. "We told him he didn't look like himself…and he really doesn't, you'll see."

"That's good to know," mumbled the professor. He fished out a set of keys from his pocket, "Well, I guess I'd better hurry over there." He started toward the front door, stopping only to grab a jacket from the hall closet. He ushered the boys out ahead of him and locked the door. "Don't worry," he said, "I'm sure I'll be able to spot him, but what do I do with him after I pick him up?"

"Keep him here, if that's okay?" Logan asked. "And my dad asked if you could call us right after and say that 'You're feeling better now', so we'll know that everything is okay."

"Absolutely, I'll remember, and you know, I think it'll be nice to have Ed here, it will give me some company, and we'll get a chance to talk. I probably have a million questions for him." The professor pulled on his jacket and started toward the driveway. "Can I drop you guys off on the way?"

"No thanks," Ben answered. "That might not be a good idea. We probably shouldn't be seen together. Besides, we have our bikes."

As soon as professor Prentiss turned onto the road, they hopped onto their bikes and sped away in the opposite direction.

CHAPTER 56

MEANWHILE, BACK AT WOLF ISLAND, Ed and his passenger pushed their boat out as far from shore as possible and climbed in. Carefully Ed guided it clear of the rocks just beneath the surface. The boat was old and not very fast, but it was still reliable and, even better, no one gave it a second look.

Ed gazed at his passenger as he steered the boat toward what once was his home. He regretted it now: he should never have given in and let *Ki* have a glimpse of what it was like to be human. She still hadn't gotten the knack of dressing like a typical teenage girl.

For a while, Ki couldn't stop talking about how humans communicated, using their vocal cords, how odd. Next, it was the smells—you could almost taste human food from the wonderful aromas that floated on the air. And the different colours that were everywhere. These humans seemed to drench themselves in the most amazing colours, even in their hair. Being among humankind was so unlike being around the Anunnaki inside the airtight complex, where everything was quiet, and gray, and where there were no smells of any kind. In contrast, the town of Milford was intoxicating, best of all, being able to watch the people, even walk among them.

Ed knew that there was no way to stop his passenger from jumping out of the boat as soon as they landed. There was no way that Ki would take the boat back to the island either. Ed had said no this time when she asked to come along, but the Anunnaki thought it was a good idea.

As they got closer to the town, Ed decided at the last moment on a change of plan. He altered course and headed toward a place he recalled from his childhood, a very old dock that he hoped might still be there.

He cared too much about her. So did John. It had quickly become a priority to keep her as far from danger as possible. The Cioth were poisoning people in Milford, yes. More people were in a coma than not. And it frightened him the way Ki stood out in the empty town. On the other hand, the island would eventually become a target. How then would the Cioth regard Ki, a half-human alien?

His passenger looked up at him, reading his mind, "Don't worry, I'll be all right. I'll be very careful."

"Huh, that's easy enough to say, but the Cioth are everywhere, and you know for a fact that you would be a target if they knew who you were."

Ed's eyes narrowed as he caught a glimpse of a modern speedboat heading toward Wolf Island. At that distance, he couldn't make out the occupant. Male, older. He held his gaze as the boat receded into the distance.

"I'll be really careful. I promise," repeated Ki.

What did *careful* really mean these days? Ed wondered, struggling to conceal the doubt from this face.

Minutes passed. The shoreline grew and small shapes began to grow into houses and trees. He had gotten his bearings. Ed smiled. It was still there. He cut the engine and drifted toward the dock. It was in terrible shape, barely standing really.

"Okay!" The answer was bright, even a little excited.

"I hope you're taking all of this seriously. Remember Ki, we consider you to be part of our family. I don't want you taking any chances."

Ki just smiled and waved, as she hopped over the side.

Moments later, Ed secured the boat as well as he could to the rickety dock. Ki was already leaping through the grass toward town.

"Take care," Ed called out, his throat tightening with emotion. He wondered if he would ever see her again.

Ki briefly held up her hand in acknowledgement and vanished in the distance.

CHAPTER 57

Scott sat back to admire his hard work. He smiled and sipped his coffee—he was pleased with himself. In spite of Ed's absence, he'd made great progress. He hadn't slept at all, but it was worth it. He didn't know when he'd get the opportunity to show Ed. And now with only one day left, and hopefully nothing unforeseen happening, the deadline could be met.

At that moment, Logan and Ben burst through the door and came to a sudden stop in front of Scott.

"What's happened?" Scott jumped up from his chair, spilling his drink.

"Hey, where is everyone?" Ed's booming voice was coming from the kitchen. A minute later, he joined them.

Ben and Logan stood there slack-jawed. They had asked Professor Prentiss to intercept Ed, but clearly this hadn't happened.

Scott looked confused, "What are you doing here, Ed? I sent the professor to keep you away from here, keep you safe. Didn't you see him at the marina?"

Ed didn't know what to say "I'm not sure what you're talking about, but I wasn't at the marina. I didn't think anyone was supposed to know that I'm alive, so why would you send the professor?

"Sorry, I know, and up until now I would have said that we were pretty safe here. I thought everyone was too busy to pay any attention to us. But we had a visit from some people in hazmat suits. And now I realize that we have to be really careful of Einhorn. You must remember him. It seems that he has declared himself the neighbourhood watch, so it's a good thing that you took the back way."

Ed rolled his eyes, "You think he reported you for something?"

"Never mind, it's stupid," Scott waved his hand dismissively. "There's something I need to show you. I just finished it a few hours ago. Want to take a look?" Scott could not help but smile.

"You mean you got it to work?" Ed eyes were wide open.

"I think it's been working all along. At least, that's my theory."

CHAPTER 58

IT WAS THE MIDDLE OF the night when Ben thought he could hear something, a soft sound in the distance. Only half awake, his fuzzy brain could not identify what it was. "Not important," he mumbled, as he rolled over and squeezed his eyes shut.

There it was again. This time, he sat up. Logan's clock read 3:30. *It has to be Logan's father*, he told himself, after all, he and Ed had been working until very late every night. All Ben had to do was go downstairs to confirm that everything was okay, and he'd be able to sleep. He rolled to his feet, and crept from the room.

In the downstairs hall, the sound was clear. Someone was at the front door, knocking very lightly. Ben tiptoed to the door and stood for a moment.

There, standing at the front door, was John McCarthy, drenched from head to foot. He pulled off his hat and shook it before stepping inside. "Is everyone asleep?" he asked Ben.

"Yes," Ben answered, looking surprised. "How come you're here? I thought it would be too dangerous."

"I know, it is, but I had to take the chance. I'm the bearer of great news." John was smiling broadly, "Let's get everyone up."

Scott and Ed charged downstairs. Logan had never seen Ed move so fast.

"Please, tell me you have good news." Scott asked anxiously.

"Is Darth okay, did the Anunnaki find a cure?" Logan looked hopeful.

"Yes!" John pointed at his grandson. "I didn't think it was ever going to happen, but they did it, and Darth is fine. Yesterday we tried the cure on him and within the hour, he was awake and moving around. Today, nobody would ever believe that he had been sick."

"So, we can wake Milford up, right, can we do it tonight?" asked an excited Logan.

"Yeah, I want to be the one to wake my parents up!" an elated Ben exclaimed.

"Wait," John said, holding up his hands. "I'm afraid we won't be waking anyone up right away. They're all safer where they are at the moment."

"What do you mean?" Logan and Ben demanded, looking puzzled.

John lowered himself onto a chair at the kitchen table. Logan could feel bad news coming.

"I know that you're disappointed, but I hope it won't be for long. The Anunnaki are afraid of what the Cioth will do if they find out the poisoning didn't work, and I have to agree with them."

"Unfortunately, I'm sure they're right." Ed said.

"The Cioth deadline is upon us, so, let's get busy." Scott gazed at the boys before turning to his father. "I have the machine put together if you want to check it out."

The three men headed for the garage, leaving the boys to themselves. At once, Logan started to take the dishes from the island and put them into the dishwasher. After, he wiped the counters clean and took out the trash.

"I know what you're doing," Ben was smiling. "It's the same reason I'll be cutting the grass at my house."

"Yeah," agreed Logan, "I want to do something for her, but also, I need something to do."

Just as the boys were heading upstairs, there was a knock on the door. Logan and Ben stared at each other for a moment.

Ben headed for the garage to warn the men while Logan waited a minute before answering the door. Professor Prentiss was just as soaked as John McCarthy had been.

"He wasn't there," said the professor. "I've been waiting all this time."

Logan slapped himself on the forehead, "Oh, geez, we forgot to call you. Ed didn't go to the marina. He landed somewhere else and got here the back way."

"Oh! I don't believe it!" The professor was looking over Logan's head. The three men were standing in front of him. The professor slumped against the wall.

CHAPTER 59

GENERAL SVENDSON WAS BEHIND HIS desk. He'd been staring at his computer screen for what seemed like hours. A fluorescent light flickered above, adding to his discomfort and mild irritation.

His back ached, too. It was just a bad habit, not taking regular breaks. His fitness watch began to vibrate and flashed the message, MOVE! Apparently, long periods of inactivity were bad for you, at least according to his watch. He stood and arched his back, hands on hips. He checked his heart rate – it had gotten down to 50 beats per minute. He wondered if this was too low and sighed. Walking downstairs for some bad coffee or sitting back down to work, neither option seemed attractive. A sharp knock at the door made the decision for him.

"Come!" roared the general.

Two men entered the room. The general recognized one of them.

"Vanderholt, isn't it? Aerial reconnaissance?"

"Yes, sir. It's Wolf Island, sir!" began Vanderholt. "This will come as a shock, sir, but one of our satellites picked up Ed Harris. We know he's supposed to be dead but there he was. Facial recognition confirmed the sighting. We have no idea where he came from, but we followed his movements all the way to the shore. He had a kid with him—maybe one of those brats from last year."

"Wait. Harris? And you say that facial recognition confirmed? How the hell did that happen? I thought he and that scientist friend of his McCarthy were both dead. They died last year."

The second man volunteered, "Yes, sir, but as you know, the power plant thing, that was our cover story. We had no idea he was still around."

"How do you explain that?" demanded the general. "We've been watching the island for a year now—covert surveillance—Corporal Stanley? Other than a report of some strange lights, it's been very quiet." He shook his head. "So our guy's been fishing off a dock, getting a tan, and we find Ed Harris by satellite?"

"One of our guys showing some initiative, sir."

"Well, it's about time. Any sign of McCarthy?" the General asked.

"No sir," replied Vanderholt.

"Well, I would have to say, where there's Ed Harris, there's John McCarthy! We'd better go over there and have a look, wouldn't you say? Get out of here and scramble the Blackhawks, now! Wolf Island! Go!"

The two men ran out the door.

The General was invigorated now. He checked his watch for his heart rate. It read 90 beats per minute.

Another figure loomed in the doorway. Trim, grey hair, brush cut. It was General James Harding.

"What the…? General Harding, welcome! I haven't seen you in a while. Not since the Wolf Island incident last year. You'll never…"

"That's quite all right, Svendson," General Harding interjected. "I'll take it from here."

Elsewhere, others were marshalling their forces. Rumour had it that it was the Russians. Time was almost up. Time to act.

CHAPTER 60

A WAVE OF *BLACKHAWK* HELICOPTERS and *Apache* gunships was just clearing the trees east of Wolf Island, and troops clad in black body armour were preparing for battle.

General Harding loved it. He surveyed the island from the right seat of his Blackhawk. It was a glorious sensation, almost like hanging over a moving cliff.

Such a fuss over this place. His thoughts flew back to that night one year ago. The night he and his half-brother, Gerald Bloch, fought for the sphere. He recalled the smells, the burning helicopter, crackling in the night air, the incredible disappearance of two men, Ed Harris and John McCarthy, into some kind of wormhole or stargate. The sphere had been torn from his grasp. He was thwarted then. He'd be better prepared this time. He'd get the sphere, no matter the cost.

He'd totally forgotten, though, about the top secret report he'd written back then, in which he'd revealed the possible presence of a wormhole on Wolf Island and its potential as a super weapon. The report had been leaked to Russia. This had unforeseen consequences.

At that very moment, two Russian missiles flew along the Fishermen's Memorial Highway at hypersonic speed, climbed briefly to 1,000 feet and dove to the target. The goal was to destroy what the Russians believed was a stargate, a threat to humanity and to Russia's status as a world power. In the blink of an eye, the missiles swept past the helicopters and struck at the heart of the island. The blast instantly filled their windscreens and swatted them from the sky.

Corporal Stanley, head of the army's surveillance team, was reading the latest spy novel, number one on the *New York Times Best Sellers* list, when he was struck by the explosion. They would find his body a week later suspended from a tree.

Meanwhile two boaters approaching the island watched in terror and disbelief as a giant cloud towered over them. In a second, the blast hit them and their boat was lifted right out of the water and deposited on the other side of the lake. It took a few minutes for them to recover their senses and witness an intense blue light arcing into the sky and out to sea, as if following the path of the Russian missiles.

* * *

Weeks later, a Russian newspaper would report that a Russian submarine, the *Emperor Vladimir Putin*, had vanished while on a training exercise in the North Atlantic.

CHAPTER 61

IT WAS MORNING. THEY HAD gathered in front of the garage. John's machine was finally ready, and just in time, the Cioth deadline was in a matter of hours. Ed, John, Scott and Professor Prentiss, had spent the last hour working together to complete the assembly. There would be no time for a field test, however. They needed to get it to the island as quickly as possible.

Birds scattered. The ground trembled slightly.

"What was that boom?" remarked Professor Prentiss.

"I don't know, but whatever it was can't be good," Scott commented. "Sounded like it came from…" He couldn't bring himself to say it.

"Could be anything. We keep going," urged John.

"How are we going to get it over there?" observed Logan, who had just emerged from the house.

"We'll take the fastest boat," John spoke. "Professor, I think that'll be yours!"

"It doesn't matter so much what we use," Scott said. "What scares me is that we'll probably be alone on the lake, with no other boats. We're going to stick out like a sore thumb."

John ran his fingers through his hair. "This is my fault," he said, crossing his arms. "We should have built the whole thing over on the island."

Scott couldn't believe what his father had said, "We couldn't do that. You know that some things were done more easily here. Besides, how could I stay on the island, with Cathy here in the hospital?

"I guess," John conceded, still hanging his head.

"Okay, next step. Let's go to the farm and get the truck, and get this thing to the marina." Scott was looking at his watch. "Shoot! Time is running out. We have to get moving."

"And we have to hope nobody notices what we're up to," Ed added, holding up crossed fingers.

* * *

John was surprised to hear that his old pick-up truck was still at the farm. Scott could never bring himself to get rid of it. "You're a good man," John said, as he hugged his son.

The old truck had a bit more rust, but with a little coaxing, it started. Precious minutes had passed since they left the house. They would need to move faster.

It was downhill from John's farm to Scott's house. The machine was sitting just inside the garage doors—they had moved it there earlier to speed things up. However, even with all four men and the two teens, it took all their strength to move the machine from the garage, load it onto the truck and secure it.

The old truck decided to be stubborn this time. It refused to start. Scott's face grew red with frustration.

"You have to be nice to her," John explained, as he nudged Scott out of the way.

John patted the dashboard and began to speak softly. "It's been a long time, old girl. I hope you missed me as much as I missed you. Now, today is really important, I need your help, so if you still have it in you…" John turned the key. The truck sputtered for a moment, started to chug, and died.

He cranked it again, uttering a silent prayer. The telltale chattering of a starter solenoid told him that his battery was almost dead. Click, click. Nothing.

He paused and pressed his forehead against the steering wheel. He sighed and for one last time, cranked the key and held it. A reluctant motor turned over, chuffed and came to life.

They arrived at the marina twelve minutes later. It was deserted. Milford was still in lockdown. John backed the truck onto the boat ramp, while the professor left to get his boat and Logan his vintage hydroplane.

Five minutes later, Scott and Ben arrived in the *Disco Volante*, just in time to help the others load the machine onto the professor's boat. Next, they covered it with a large tarp.

At last, three unlikely boats emerged from the harbour, the wooden-hulled Disco Volante, the professor's sleek speedboat, and Logan's tiny hydroplane. It was a gamble, a shell game really. Only one of the boats carried the all-important cargo, the machine, but all were draped in tarps. Three boats moved in tight formation at 50 miles per hour, and in no time the island was in sight.

* * *

Even so, luck would desert them minutes out from Wolf Island. A Cioth patrol craft swooped down and skimmed across the waves at lightning speed on a collision course. It flew so low that everybody aboard the three boats ducked.

The craft turned about and began its attack run. In scant seconds, it was skimming just behind Logan's boat.

Scott peeled off to the left to draw off the attacker but the ruse failed, and the spacecraft remained in lock step behind Logan.

By now, the tarp aboard Logan's boat had almost broken loose and was slapping violently in the breeze. Logan tore at the last ties securing the tarp to his boat and released it into the breeze. In an instant, the tarp billowed and enveloped the Cioth craft.

Blinded, the alien craft came to a dead stop. The tarp glowed, glowed red, glowed white and caught fire, and dropped in flaming shreds to the water.

The tarp had bought them precious seconds. Scott veered right and resumed his position in the convoy, behind the professor.

Logan took up a position behind his father and in moments, the spacecraft was upon him. Logan throttled back and broke left. The Cioth craft overshot Logan's boat and swung around to press the attack.

As the three boats emerged from the shelter of the bay, the lake was churning with large, rolling waves. Their boats shot across them, pitching up and down, blasting through stinging plumes of spray as they went.

Logan turned his head to see a fierce, blue laser light cut his boat in half, and he tumbled into the green surf and foam.

He was drowning. Seconds passed. A hand drove down and yanked him out of the water. It was his dad. Logan gasped for air. Ben gave him a high-five.

With the Disco Volante stopped cold to pick up Logan, the professor's boat was alone. A Cioth materialized on the deck. The professor looked back in sheer terror as it advanced. He spun the wheel hard to knock the alien off his feet.

The island grew large and the professor thought he saw a lone figure on a bluff ahead. The figure, clad in black, raised two arms. One held a lantern.

The Disco Volante surged forward, with Scott at the wheel, Ben and Logan standing close behind him. It closed quickly on the professor's craft.

"Where is it? The gun, the gun! What did you do with it?" yelled Logan.

Ben was dumbfounded. Seconds passed and it dawned on him, he had the gun. He seized the weapon from his jacket, pointed and fired towards the Cioth aboard the professor's boat. Nothing. He pressed again, nothing.

"Oh my God, it's keyed to my DNA," Logan yelled. "Give it to me!"

Ben fumbled for the weapon and dropped it. Their faces fell.

Within those fleeting seconds, a white light shot from the island, and where the Cioth once stood, a collapsing black hole. The pursuing spacecraft peeled off and retreated.

The figure in black waved to them. They waved back, relieved, and steered toward the light.

Still, something seemed odd. Part of the rock beneath the bluff was in dark shadow, and the closer they came, the darker the shadow got.

"Crap," yelled Ben, as he pointed at the shore. "Is that what I think it is?"

"Whoa! This is great!" Logan yelled back, as he fist-punched the air. "It's a tunnel!"

Scott stood up, still gripping the steering wheel. He began to laugh.

The tunnel swelled open, and the professor's boat coasted inside.

For the *Disco Volante* perhaps, it was too late. The deadline to surrender the sphere was now. From above, more Cioth ships swooped down and chased the boat, surrounding it. Fierce explosions hit the water all around causing large waves that threatened to swamp them. As Scott tried to move away, a shot would land in their path, forcing them to slow down and stop. Now one of ships had taken a position directly above the boat.

Scott tightened his grip on the wheel, took a deep breath and yelled as loud as he could. One, two, three, he jammed the throttle to full power. The front of the boat leapt up as the boat surged forward. Logan and Ben were thrown onto the back seat. A ball of light from the alien ship flew toward them and exploded behind the boat. Scott and the boys glanced over their shoulders. They were still alive! Successive flashes came at a frantic pace, on and on, always exploding over and behind them, as if hitting a wall.

"There must be a force field!" Scott realized, awestruck. Then came the tunnel.

CHAPTER 62

BEN SQUEEZED HIS EYES SHUT in disbelief. He opened them. The tunnel had given way to a giant cave with a jetty on one side and brilliant lights over head. Other craft bobbed in the dissipating wake. There was the professor's boat, being secured by some Anunnaki. The professor was reclining on the jetty, breathless, stunned.

Logan jumped onto the jetty with Ben and spotted a small, black-suited figure wearing a black helmet and gloves. "There he is, the guy on the bluff who guided us in!"

The boys headed over, but to their surprise, the stranger retreated. He was shorter than they expected, convincing the two that the stranger was Anunnaki. They ran to catch up. "We just wanted to thank you," Ben called out.

"Yeah," agreed Logan, "That was so cool!"

Logan extended his hand toward the stranger.

The stranger stared down at Logan's hand before nodding politely and removing his helmet. A cascade of black hair tumbled out from beneath. The boys were speechless when they saw her face. It was the girl from the marina, the one who rode an old bike and wore baggy clothes.

"It's you again!" Ben exclaimed, "What are you doing here?"

"I live here," she whispered to Ben, "just like you used to."

CHAPTER 63

BEN STARED BACK. HE COULDN'T imagine what the strange girl meant.

"What are you talking about?" asked Logan. "Ben has lived in Milford ever since he was a kid."

"Yeah, that's right," agreed Ben, crossing his arms.

"I mean before that." The girl hadn't taken her eyes off Ben's face. "You are my DNA match."

"What's that supposed to mean?" Ben shot back. "I don't know what you are talking about!"

"She's right," John McCarthy had come up behind them. "I wish we had time to explain this, but unfortunately it will have to wait."

Behind him, Ed was supervising the offloading of the machine from the professor's boat. Two Anunnaki, wearing dark, mechanically enhanced suits, lifted it and handed it to two others who were standing on the jetty. Logan couldn't believe it. It had taken the six of them to load the machine onto Grampa's truck.

The heavy machine now sat on a circle etched into the floor. One of the Anunnaki tapped on the edge of the circle with his foot. The circle rose up to reveal a floating disk and the Anunnaki pushed the machine along the jetty toward a large opening as though it weighed nothing. John and the girl followed.

All this time the boys could hear explosions pounding against the force field outside. "I think they're going crazy," Logan said.

"Yes, I'm afraid you're right," John agreed, "They probably thought that the poisoning would be enough to convince me to give up the sphere."

All the occupants of the cave looked up sharply as a particularly close hit rocked the cave and knocked them off their feet.

"This is unexpected," observed one of the Anunnaki, while the others nodded in agreement. "They have developed stronger weapons."

"Come on you two, let's go!" Ed pushed the boys forward, attempting to steer them toward the opening. "We have to leave here. We'll be safer down below."

They hurried toward the end of the jetty. As the boys passed through the opening, they noticed how thick the door was. It slid into place with a heavy thud and locked behind them.

"That's Anunnaki steel," said Ed with a smile as he rapped his knuckles hard against the door. "Nineteen inches thick. It's impenetrable."

Ahead was a corridor hewn out of solid rock. It went on as far as the eye could see. At intervals, more heavy doors closed behind them. These resembled bank vault doors.

When they reached their destination and the door whooshed open, there were Scott, John, and the strange girl, surrounded by a number of Anunnaki. The room was a hive of activity.

John looked over at Ed and nodded toward Scott, "He needs some help."

Ed hurried over to help Scott and two of the Anunnaki who were pushing something that looked like a large laser cannon to the front of the machine.

"This doesn't look like just a machine, Dad," Scott shot a glance at his father. "It looks like a weapon to me!"

"I know, sorry. We decided that we couldn't tell you. It was safer for you if you believed you were making a machine that would detect alien DNA. We figured that anyone would believe that because of the work you do, especially that nosy neighbour of yours. Besides, with the health department and the police both looking for a crazy person who is poisoning the whole town, we didn't want you to act suspiciously."

All the Anunnaki looked up at the same time as the lights in the room blinked three times.

"That was a warning!" Ed yelled.

"We have to connect the machine to the power source," John called over his shoulder as he worked beside Teaf. "We're out of time now. The Cioth must have broken through."

Logan moved closer to his father, "Yeah, but even if they did, we still have to be okay, right? I heard all those doors closing behind us in the passage." Logan sounded hopeful as he turned to Ed, "They can't get through Anunnaki steel. You said it was impenetrable."

Off in the distance, a loud screeching sound put everyone on edge. Something dreadful was trying to penetrate the first door.

"It sounds like it won't be long before they've broken through," John stated, glancing up briefly from his work.

The Anunnaki moved to a corner of the room. They knew that they were not supposed to interfere in any way, but how had things changed so dramatically? How had the Cioth become so powerful without them knowing?

"You know what's happened," Ed said, glancing their way. "The Cioth must have stolen a weapon from somewhere."

Silence. Ben and Logan held their breath.

They hadn't noticed that the girl was now standing very close behind them. "Can you feel it yet?" she asked, tugging on Ben's sleeve.

"Feel what?" he asked innocently.

"You know what I mean, the vibration in your head. Mine has just started."

"No, I don't know what you're talking about," Ben looked away to put some distance between them.

Louder, it was the screeching sound of metal dying and doors falling; and silence.

"It must have happened to you," the girl was more insistent as she tried to move in front of Ben.

"What is this, do you think you're my girlfriend or something?" Ben was trying to embarrass her, so that she might leave him alone.

Logan had been watching the men work, but hearing Ben's remark, lashed out, "Look, just because you saved us doesn't mean that you're one of us, you know!"

Ed was only a few feet away, his eyes narrowed. He shot the boys a scathing look. "Leave her alone! You'd better be nice to her, she's Ben's sister."

CHAPTER 64

FOR THE MOMENT, THEY COULD breathe. The assault had stopped. It was the calm before the storm. The Cioth had pierced most of the doors. How many were left, how much time did they have?

The Anunnaki were still huddled together. Their communication at this point did not include the humans, but John could guess what they were thinking. He prayed that they had a plan in case of invasion.

"We have to move this weapon to the surface," John said with great urgency.

"Right," Ed answered, "I only wish it could help us with those devils breaking down the doors."

"What about the sphere? I'll bet it could stop them," said Logan, looking hopeful.

"The sphere is powerful, but quite unpredictable," John explained.

Ki had her arms crossed as she stepped in front of Ben, "You must feel the vibrations now!"

Ben looked angry as he pulled the girl away from the others, "Okay, I do." he admitted, "So what?"

"We can help them all. Have you used it yet?"

Ben was dumbfounded. He stared at her while he thought for a moment, "Well, yeah, I guess so," he whispered. "I zapped a couple of Cioth who were going to kill my friend."

Ki broke into a smile, "I knew it, and you saw me use it on the Cioth."

"That was really you on the bluff?" Ben's eyebrows shot up. "You can just use it when you want to?"

"Of course," she looked surprised.

"Well, when I did it, I didn't know how it happened. I couldn't figure out how I did it."

CHAPTER 65

As the door opened to the elevator that would take them to the surface, the sphere emerged. It went directly to John, hovering above and behind him.

John gave Ed a knowing look.

"Umm, right... I think we should all tread carefully here," Ed murmured softly. He tried to smile. "We don't want our friend here," he looked up at the sphere, "to sense our fear and overreact. It might be tempted to open up another wormhole and send us who knows where. We could even end up on another planet, and we wouldn't be any use to anyone here."

Ki was the last to board the elevator. They were all surprised when, after the doors closed, she began to hum.

Logan listened to her for a moment and smiled. "Nice," he said. "Only happy people hum, right, people who aren't afraid." He began to hum along.

"I don't recognize the tune, but I like the idea," said Scott, before joining in. Soon all the humans were humming, and smiling.

The Anunnaki on board tilted their heads as they listened to the strange noise. "Why are humans always so noisy?"

Logan and Ben kept checking the sphere. It was a relief to see that its colour had not changed. If they remembered correctly, red was the colour that they didn't want to see.

It was only four minutes, but it felt much longer before the doors opened again. This time they were in a large, gray hangar. Two alien ships sat side by side. They were sometimes blue, sometimes white, depending on the light. Behind the ships stood the cannon, which had evidently been moved in a separate elevator.

Scott was awestruck. "Wow, look at this stuff!" he whispered as he followed behind Logan. Father and son looked at each other in disbelief.

The machine, John's contribution, was already installed on the cannon. John climbed to the top of the cannon with the sphere behind him. He placed the sphere into a receptacle. Thus installed, the sphere's enormous energy could power the gun.

At that moment, a horrifying sound grabbed their attention. The elevator doors were being torn to shreds.

"As soon as they come through those doors, we can use the cannon to blast them," Scott yelled over to his father.

"No, we can't. It's far too powerful to be used in here," John called back.

"He's right, this whole place would collapse," Ed confirmed.

Remnants of the doors exploded into the room. They took shelter behind the spaceships, except John. He was still atop the weapon, lying very still, when a dozen Cioth walked calmly into the room.

They were dressed like soldiers, covered from head to toe in black armour, and carrying heavy weapons strapped to their shoulders and braced the length of their arms.

Ben hunkered down, he could hardly move, the buzzing in his head was intense.

Ki was pressed against the side of the ship. She whispered to him, "We can do this Ben, we can stop them," she quietly urged. "Help me."

"Why do you keep asking me?" Ben hissed, glaring at her. "You don't need me. You took out those other guys by yourself."

"That was different. There are too many of them now, and my power will run out. You have to help!"

Ben turned to face her. His face grew red, with ears pulled back and chin extended. "I'm telling you, I don't know how I did it, okay?"

A fusillade of pulsed light tore over their heads, cracking like thunder as it ripped through the air.

"You've already done it," Ki said. "You must have felt the energy when it ran down your arm and left through your hand. That's all there is to it."

The Cioth had spotted John and the sphere at the top of the cannon. Five of the armed aliens began to climb. John placed his hand on the sphere.

Scott gasped and got to his feet.

"No, don't be crazy!" Ed told him as he grabbed Scott and held him back.

"Listen to me," Ki whispered, "all you have to do is let the power escape. You just push it out from your core, your belly. Come on… try it!"

Two of the Cioth approached John. The sphere began to glow red.

"No, no, no!" Ed screamed as he dropped his head into his hands.

"Okay! Here goes," Ben raised his hand and aimed in the direction of one of the Cioth. He inhaled a big gulp of air, and then roared a loud, "NO!" A tingling sensation travelled down his arm. It was so strong it made his arm shake. A flash shot from his hand, ball lightning that grew larger before hitting its target and imploding into a black hole and dust.

Ki sent a blast that took out the Cioth closest to John. Ben, now reassured, blasted another.

Across the room, the Cioth stood dazed, taken aback by a weapon they hadn't seen before. Then, a shift, steel in their spines, fire in their eyes, they swarmed into the room and resumed their relentless assault on the cannon.

Ki was shaking her head as she scrambled to her feet. A primal growl rose deep from her belly.

"Stay down!" Ed yelled.

She dashed in front of the ship, and stood facing the Cioth. "Hey!" she yelled, waving her arms, trying to draw attention to herself. The men behind the ship jumped up and started to run, anything to distract the aliens.

A second later, Ben was by Ki's side A second after that, the room erupted in a firestorm. White flashes and black holes filled the room. Ki and Ben dropped to the floor and rolled in opposite directions where they disappeared into a white fog.

Ed, Scott and Logan lay with their faces pressed against the floor.

A thick, silvery cloud lingered. None of the humans made a move. Out of an oppressive silence, they could make out a moaning voice. But who was it? It sounded human. At last, they recognized Ben's voice.

The cloud had cleared enough that they could make out Ben, rubbing his foot. "I think I twisted my ankle."

"Did you see that?" Logan asked. He dropped to his knees beside his friend. "Was that you?" his friend asked.

Ben shrugged.

CHAPTER 66

JOHN CLIMBED DOWN FROM THE cannon to inspect the damage. After a few nervous minutes, he was satisfied that the weapon was still intact. However, he couldn't say much for the room. It was a mess, with large chunks of rock all over the floor and strange piles of dust here and there.

The most important thing now, John knew, was to get the weapon outside. At the same time, the Anunnaki were working to re-establish the force field above the facility. John remembered that their main goal was to avoid any conflict with the Cioth, so he was shocked when Deefin remained by the humans, as if ready to help. He was donning one of the exoskeleton suits that would enable him to carry the cannon.

Deefin drew closer to John, gazing at his fellow Anunnaki, and said quietly, "They can't believe what is happening. So much violence… and the Cioth have vastly improved their weaponry. We were not prepared for this."

"I saw that, but why are you willing to help us?" John asked. "Doesn't it go against the rules?"

"The reason is because I am not surprised or curious about the Cioth or their improvements. I'm just afraid for all humans and afraid for the universe. The Cioth will continue to be violent unless they are stopped. I want to help you to stop them."

With that, Deefin crouched and lifted the giant cannon over his head. "Where do you wish this placed, John?"

In minutes, John and Deefin were on the surface. The sterile atmosphere of the Anunnaki base beneath the island gave way to what was above—the colour and scent of fall.

It dawned on John that the entire island had been protected from the missile attacks, though part of the mainland wasn't so fortunate. He could see a line of broken trees to the east, the remains of what appeared to be helicopters, and other wreckage floating in the lake. Ed and Scott stood nearby, aghast at the devastation. The teens had stayed underground—Logan and Ki had insisted on looking after Ben and his twisted ankle.

"At least the town seems to have been spared," Scott murmured.

John squinted into the clear blue sky. Twenty white dots. They were visible to the naked eye. Cioth ships.

"Over there," John called to Deefin, pointing at a treeless knoll and it was done, the cannon placed on the ground. Deefin bowed curtly and stepped away.

John leapt onto the platform and aimed the weapon high into space. A planet-smashing mass loomed overhead. At that very moment, John fired the weapon. The sphere grew red, then white-hot. The ground shook, a grunting sound followed, and a fiery white pulse shot upwards.

Observers would later recount the sight, a collision between an immovable object and an irresistible force.

High above the earth, at the edge of space, the two met. At the curve of the earth's atmosphere, it grew black and for one minute, a queer darkness fell on the planet, like a solar eclipse.

A second grunting eruption spewed from the weapon, a fiery pulse, and in the murderous cold of space, the fleet of Cioth ships simply disappeared.

The sphere with its unlimited power, coupled with John's machine, had smashed the entire fabric of space occupied by the Cioth fleet. Space and time were bent into nothingness, along with twenty ships.

The blue sky reasserted itself.

"Yes!" yelled John, pumping his first into the air. He turned to the sphere, but to his dismay, it appeared lifeless.

CHAPTER 67

BEN AND THE OTHERS BEGAN to emerge from the Anunnaki base.

John gazed deep into the clear, blue sky arcing overhead. The sphere had sacrificed itself for them. It was bittersweet. He bit his lower lip and nodded.

Deefin caught Logan's eye and pointed at an old crop-duster airplane off in the distance, circling Milford.

Logan paused. It was odd because all commercial air traffic had been suspended for some time and the skies had grown ominously quiet. Now, long white trails of cloud drifted across the sky and broke up, falling to the ground.

People in town also saw the clouds. They had heard the twin boom of the missile attack on Wolf Island. They had seen the awesome alien pulse from the island. They were afraid.

Time passed though. Over the next few days, people would awaken. The people who were infected last would recover first, while the others took longer. The Anunnaki had indeed cracked the secret of the Cioth poison, the antidote worked.

CHAPTER 68

THE FIRST SATURDAY OF OCTOBER, three families headed to Wolf Island. It was a fine day, cloudless, sunny and mild. The lake was mirror smooth.

Aboard the *Disco Volante* and the professor's boat were Katy, Darcy, Ben and Logan, as well as Logan's and Ben's parents. Darcy's mother and father were absent—Darcy had informed everyone that his parents were too upset to deal with aliens.

An hour later, beneath a familiar bluff, a familiar tunnel began to materialize. Ben's father sprang up and stayed standing until they were well inside.

On the jetty inside were John, Ed and Ki, smiling and waving.

"So where are the aliens?" Darcy asked as he climbed out of the boat.

Ben and Ki exchanged glances.

"They've left," Ed called back. "Too much has happened here. It made them nervous."

Darcy looked stunned, "Are you kidding? I don't believe it. I've missed everything!"

"Well, not everything," John corrected, as he waved an arm at their surroundings. "This is a pretty impressive facility; we thought you might enjoy a tour of the place."

CHAPTER 69

IN A SMALL, GREY ROOM next to the conference room, a rising chorus of voices, visitors in awe of the sights, could be heard through the door.

A glass case containing the sphere sat on a pedestal in the middle of the room. A spotlight was its only illumination. The once brilliant sphere was now almost indistinguishable from the colour of the room.

If anyone were listening, it wouldn't have been difficult to pick out John McCarthy's strong, confident voice from the others next door. The deep baritone seemed to awaken something in the sphere. In a matter of moments, a warm, radiant light bathed the room in brilliant yellow.

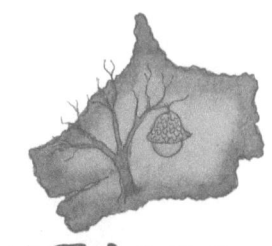

ABOUT THE AUTHORS

A. M. Neilly is a creative writer, fine artist and illustrator.

M. R. Neilly is a freelance writer.

Growing up, both were ardent fans of teen novels. *Wolf Island Mysteries II* is their second in the *Wolf Island Mysteries* series. Both firmly believe that reading at an early age has enriched their lives and stimulated their imaginations.

www.ingramcontent.com/pod-product-compliance
Lightning Source LLC
LaVergne TN
LVHW041626060526
838200LV00040B/1451